ELLISON BAY

A NOVEL

By Jerry Price & Tom Roy

ELLISON BAY

ISBN: 978-0-9765412-6-4

© 2017 by Jerry Price and Tom Roy
2BRealMen Publishing
jerry@2BRealMen.com & tom@2BRealMen.com

What Others Are Saying

Jerry Price is so unlike any other born again Christian man I have ever met. He teams up with Tom Roy where they demand your attention as writers, because of deeply felt beliefs in their journey of life. That journey has impacted their ability to put down on paper, words and thoughts of every man's struggles from the cradle to the grave. Is this story, a story of your life? It could be every man's untold story.

- CHUCK RAMSAY
Former News Anchor for Channel 2 News in Green Bay, WI.

It's been said that many of us spend our adulthood getting over our childhood. Most end up with Father issues and generational sins, which keep popping up because we don't examine why we do what we do.

In the second book of their trilogy, Jerry and Tom have done a great job of illustrating how men can spend years trying to figure out how to be a real man, instead of only modeling what they saw growing up. I've enjoyed both books and following the lives of their characters, Bob and Lois; as they try to fill up the massive holes left by the loss of their son and past issues never dealt with. Many of the Athletes I serve have had to deal with these issues and I believe will benefit from this book.

- DON CHRISTENSEN
Executive VP. Professional Athlete division
Ronald Blue and Co.

Ellison Bay, just like it's predecessor Sandusky Bay, is a brutally honest story that is not afraid to be real with its reader. The struggles Bob Chadwick endures are powerfully real and heart wrenching. The book is not afraid to illustrate the struggles of men or provide the only answer to overcome those struggles, a personal relationship with Jesus Christ.

- JOSEPH DOUGHERTY
College Senior

Tom Roy and Jerry Price have written a book, which I recommend as a must read for anyone going through difficult trials in their lives. That I believe is all of us. I found myself rooting for Bob Chadwick throughout his very difficult journey, as we watch him try almost everything he can to soften the blows. It made me think about a number of people I know trying everything but turning their life over to Christ— only to continue to struggle.

ELLISON BAY will also make most readers want to come to Door County, Wisconsin. It's a beautiful place from a state I call home. Go Packers!

- MIKE McGIVERN
Host of Faith in the Zone Radio Show Sports Radio 1057 FM
The Fan Milwaukee

When Tom Roy and Jerry Price get together, I love to sit and listen. When they write a book, I love to read it! Ellison Bay is another great book from this writing team. I am fascinated by the journey of the characters we were introduced to in Sandusky Bay, and I loved meeting the new people in this book. I thoroughly enjoyed Ellison Bay and I can't wait to see what comes next!

- DR. TED BARRETT
Major League Umpire

Ellison Bay 5

An irrefutable read that leaves readers without dispute!

- DELVYN CRAWFORD
Author, Speaker, Family Fatherhood Life Coach
Founder Gutter Enterprises

JERRY PRICE & TOM ROY

FOREWORD

A man's life never unfolds like we expect, and co-authors Jerry Price and Tom Roy give you a glimpse into the *real* world of selfishness, missed expectations and a cascading series of events that bring reality front and center. Hold on as you dig into one man's story, his dreams, his pain and what it means to get a taste for an authentic journey toward manhood.

Whether you're in your early 20's and laying out *plans* for your life, or in the later part of life and reflecting on how time has gone by; this book hits to the core.

Who am I really? What am I really capable of? What do I really want to do, and do I really know how to find the greatest sense of fulfillment?

If we're honest with ourselves, in the highs and lows, we're in a lot less control of the outcomes than we'd like to admit. However, we are in control of how we choose to respond to life and what we take responsibility for. We know we want more and we want it to last but why can't we grasp it?

Every guy needs to be asking himself the tough questions, if he hopes to find real life and not regret. But is he too afraid? Too self centered? Is he fooling himself with an *as soon as...* an, *I could but...* or, maybe an *if only...*?

JERRY PRICE & TOM ROY

Bob Chadwick's story just might crack open some of these questions. But prepare yourself. The answers might be tougher than you think.

- Mike Morford
CEO & Founder eFormed Partners

PROLOGUE

Bob Chadwick felt paralyzed. On the outside he was in shock, but inside he was a war zone of memories, regrets and dread. Big decisions lay ahead of him and he needed to pull himself together.

Memories of his dad, Sam Chadwick, flooded Bob's mind. He had never really grieved after his father unexpectedly passed three years earlier. Yes, he read the letter Sam gave to him just before his death, but Bob put the letter away without giving it deeper thought.

Joey, Bob's son, had just graduated from high school and signed a pro baseball contract with the Chicago White Sox. Bob's relationship with his son was finally improving. As a graduation gift, Bob planned a Canadian fishing vacation with him, but what was supposed to be a dream trip ended in a tragedy.

Bob now faced the painful task of returning to his wife without Joey. How would he explain the drowning? It was too much! He questioned if he had what it took to survive his grief, let alone console Lois. Bob Chadwick knew he needed help.

The Chadwick story continues from Sandusky Bay, Ohio to Ellison Bay, Wisconsin as he sorts out what it means to be a responsible man.

Tom Roy
President and Founder of the UPI, Inc
Ministry to Major League Baseball Players
Author of Released

Ellison Bay 9

A Story Of God's Power Released In Pro Baseball
Co-Author with Jerry Price of Sandusky Bay and Ellison Bay
Co-Founder of 2BRealMen Initiative

JERRY PRICE & TOM ROY

1

"The most painful thing is losing someone who
was always beside you...!"
kawthar koukou

It was mid-June, 1973, and Bob Chadwick found himself driving into the Canadian town of Denbigh, located in the Addington Highlands township of Ontario. A community of about 1500 people, Denbigh was the closest town to Bob's cabin at Lake Weslemkoon.

Bob parked and walked slowly toward the front entrance of the Royal Canadian Police Station, noticing the large Canadian Flag flying high on a post attached to the building. Old-world on the outside, this village station seemed to symbolize Denbigh, a jewel of Addington County, with boating, fishing and hiking in unspoiled wilderness.

But once inside, Bob only saw drab tile floors and gray metal desks, like many police stations across the continent. It smelled of mimeograph ink and stale coffee.

The receptionist was cool but polite. "How can I help you, eh?"

"My name is Bob Chadwick. I'm here to see Sergeant Ben Smith."

"Yes, Mr. Chadwick. I'm sorry to hear of your loss," she said.

"Hear of my loss?" Bob thought. It sounded like she was referring to nothing more than losing a softball game at a picnic!

"You're talking about my son!" Bob wanted to shout his rage at her.

Taking a breath to steady his self, Bob managed to respond calmly. "Thank you ma'am."

He took a seat facing a huge door leading to the commander's office while he waited for his appointment. His purpose for being there was to identify his son's body.

Bob hadn't slept. His mind was trying to make sense of the events of the past few days. How could Joey be gone? Just two days ago he and his son were having such great times fishing on Lake Weslemkoon. Was it all a cruel nightmare?

"Oh God! This is my fault. I should never have left him alone on the dock after dark! I can't handle this," he thought.

Bob was in anguish. How does one endure the pain of losing an only son? Why, when things were finally improving, did life take such a terrible turn? When would this wrenching pain ever release its grip?

* * *

Just then the Detachment Commander walked in.

"Mr. Chadwick?" he said. "I'm Sergeant Smith."

The sergeant was a large, plainspoken man. Bob could hear the leather of his holster creak as the man walked toward him.

"I'm very sorry, Mr. Chadwick. Don't know what else to say."

In Bob's mind, that was all he needed to say. He was in no mood for chatter.

"Please follow me." Sergeant Smith said.

The Commander opened a swinging gate that led toward a second door. Bob paused and took a deep breath, knowing inside that room would be the lifeless body of his son.

Sergeant Smith asked kindly, "You need a little more time?"

Bob took a breath and responded. "No. I'm ready."

Three steps inside the door Bob saw the gurney with the white sheet. He began to tremble involuntarily as they walked toward the cart.

The commander pulled back the crisp white sheet. "Is this your son?" he asked?

Bob couldn't breathe. Joey's body was pale and stiff, his life gone. His body still carried the nasty burn marks from when Joey was just a little boy. In a moment of anger, Bob had accidentally spilled hot coffee on his son.

It was too much. Bob did his best to keep his emotions in check but pain overtook him. He fell to his knees, broken and sobbing.

Sergeant Smith had two boys of his own and couldn't imagine what Bob was going through. He placed a hand on Bob's shoulder and waited patiently.

After several minutes Bob struggled to his feet, his spirit crushed. Feebly, he managed to say, "Yes that's my son."

Staring at Joey's body, Bob noticed something else. There were no other marks on Joey. No cuts, scratches or bruises.

"Commander, what happened to my boy? I know Joey was found in the lake, but he was an excellent swimmer. I don't see any injuries."

"We don't know yet, Mr. Chadwick. The coroner will do the autopsy today. We've ordered an investigation."

Sergeant Smith continued. "There are a number of reasons autopsies are performed. The main reasons are to determine the medical cause of death and to gather evidence if needed in a court of law. We should have some answers within the next few days."

Now that the body had been identified, the sergeant covered Joey's body and signaled that the two men should leave the room. Bob felt ripped in half. Part of him couldn't leave quickly enough and the other part couldn't bear to leave his son.

* * *

Bob filled out the few forms at the station desk, pushed back his chair and stood.

"So this is it? How do I take my son home to Ohio for a proper burial?"

"Normally we try to release the deceased to a funeral home within one or two days. If there are more questions or if we determine foul play was involved, it may take longer. Do you have the name of the funeral home in your town?" the sergeant asked.

Bob was caught off guard.

"No sir, haven't had to visit one of those for a long time. Can I call you when I get back to the states?"

"Sure. That's fine." Sergeant Smith answered. "After we get the autopsy results and the death certificate, we'll have your son's body flown into the airport closest to your town and arrange for the funeral home to recover the body. They will sign the certificate and take care of all the regulations with your government."

Bob thanked Sergeant Smith and left the outpost. Even through his fog of despair, he didn't envy the difficult position of law enforcement. The job required a lot more than writing speeding tickets.

* * *

As Bob returned to his car, he tried to identify his feelings about what just happened. He knew it was necessary to fill out forms and identify the body but it all seemed so cold and impersonal to him. He felt numb.

Driving back to the lake cabin, Bob could feel the lack of sleep catching up with him. Reality was beginning to hit and it felt like a knife in his gut. He stopped at a local grocery to pick up some *Southern Comfort,* just in case he needed some help making it through the night ahead. *"Southern Comfort for my northern pain,"* he thought bitterly.

Back at the cabin, Bob began packing Joey's clothes and fishing gear. Each item held memories. Even dirty socks seemed sacred. As Bob stuffed his son's belongings into the duffle bag, the task grew unbearable. Angrily, he threw it against the wall.

"Why, God? Why has this happened to my son?"

Bob flung himself on Joey's sleeping cot and wept, eventually crying himself into a deep sleep. Sometime during the night he woke, still feeling the stabbing pain. It felt like Joey should be walking through the door any minute! How could this be real? His thoughts turned to the trip home. Suddenly he realized he hadn't talked with Lois for more than a day. *"What must she be thinking?"* he wondered.

He got up and walked across the room, guessing what time it was. It didn't matter. Nothing mattered. He gave up and grabbed the bottle he had purchased earlier. The next thing he remembered was waking up around ten the next morning, fighting through a pounding hangover.

After several mugs of coffee, Bob packed his car for the eleven- hour drive home. As he picked up Joey's new fishing tackle box, a blind rage came over him. He grabbed the box and ran down to the pier, launching it into the lake with a long, loud moan. He stood there, motionless, watching the rings of water.

JERRY PRICE & TOM ROY

Something about that felt good, for an instant. Too bad it didn't last. He turned to face the long trip home.

*   *   *

The long, gravel road that led from the cabin to the main highway passed through a campground. Bob saw a phone booth and pulled over to try giving Lois a call. There was no answer and he speculated where she could be.

Bob decided to call a neighbor he barely knew but was a good friend to Lois.

"Hello, the Haid residence," a kind voice answered.

"Hi Helen, this is Bob Chadwick. I've tried to call Lois but there's no answer. Do you know where she might be?"

There was a dead silence on the other end. Finally Helen spoke.

"Lois came over last evening to talk. She's not doing well. I took her to the hospital and they admitted her. Bob, she needs you to be home. I know this will be hard for you to hear but she tried to take her life this morning."

"What! Is she ok?" Bob asked.

"She's in stable condition, Helen said, but needs you. Please hurry home."

"Thanks for helping out, Helen. I'll be there as soon as I can."

Reeling from this news, Bob hung up the phone and headed back to his car. He turned on the ignition and set out toward the highway, heading back to Sandusky Bay.

God! How do I deal with this? What do I say to Lois?

2

"The truth is rarely pure and never simple."
Oscar Wilde, The Importance of Being Earnest

It was a clear, sunny Canadian morning. But a front was moving into the Addington Highlands as Bob began the long drive to Ohio.

Just twenty-four hours earlier he had been at the Denbigh police station to identify his son's body. His head was already pounding from pouring out his pain and anger the night before. The change in the weather was causing sinus pressure, adding to his headache. A bit too much Southern Comfort may have also contributed to his discomfort.

"Great," thought Bob, bitterly. *"Just what I needed! One more thing to deal with!" My only son is gone, my wife tried to kill herself and here I am with a damn killer headache! How am I supposed to get through this?"*

Everything in Bob's life was upside down and he wondered if anything would ever get back to normal, whatever that meant. For now, he felt like a wet towel being rung out by a four hundred pound NFL lineman. As he drove through the Canadian wilderness, Bob grew disconnected from the beauty around him. It all seemed meaningless and fragile, much like his life.

* * *

As the miles rolled on toward Ohio, Bob's mind took him back to the day he first met Lois in Coaltown, West Virginia. She was at the general store getting ingredients for her Southern pound cake. She dipped the scoop into the flour bin and as she turned to empty the flour into her tin, they collided, covering both of them in flour.

"Whoa!" he said, too late, with only their eyes being visible.

Embarrassed, Lois apologized, trying to brush flour off both of them. "Oh, I'm sorry! I'm so sorry!" she said. Bob started to laugh at her and she returned the laughter.

"I'm Bob Chadwick," he said. "You look like a ghost."

"I'm Lois Struthers, she said, "and you look like a Christmas tree covered in snow."

After a brief conversation, Lois invited Bob over for pound cake to make up for her snowfall of flour covering him.

"In fact," she offered, "would you like to come for dinner? We're having fried chicken, potato salad and collard greens. We'll have my southern pound cake for dessert." That was an invitation Bob couldn't refuse.

"That's a mighty fine offer," Bob laughed, "but I reckon I'll clean up first!" After a few more shared laughs, they left, anticipating seeing each other again.

The thunderstorm that had been threatening hit suddenly and pulled Bob's thoughts back to the present when he saw signs for Cloyne, a small town on highway 41 about an hour from Lake Weslemkoon. He tried to hang onto the pleasant memory of that day in Coaltown, but darker memories of the pain he caused Lois through the years of their marriage crowded his mind. And now, she was waiting for him in a Sandusky hospital on a suicide watch.

* * *

JERRY PRICE & TOM ROY

With effort, Bob directed his mind back to fishing with his son, which was one event he recalled like it was yesterday.

It was the summer before Joey entered high school and baseball was over for the season. Joey was bored and Bob decided to distract him with fishing.

"Son, get in the car," he commanded. "Okay dad. What's up?"

"I hear some fish calling your name but first we have a little shopping to do."

Bob stopped at a sporting goods store and Joey entered without knowing what to expect. His dad, however, knew exactly what to look for as he headed toward the fishing gear.

"Here, son, this pole is just like mine. You should catch some real lunkers on this thing," Bob said.

Joey grabbed the cane pole, loving the feel of it in his hand. "I think you're right, dad. This one will work great!"

Suddenly, Bob's memories were interrupted. A deer leaped in front of his car, nearly missing the front bumper! Seeing deer cross the highway in mid-June didn't make sense to him. The corn was just sprouting in the farm fields and deer usually stayed away until the fall.

As the pleasant memory dissolved, a wave of sadness washed over Bob. It had stirred a great sense of pride in his son. At the same time, he realized he had failed his son in many ways. The drinking.

The pornography in the shed. Failing to show up at baseball games. The way he had treated Lois in front of his son. And more.

Regret overwhelmed Bob and he began to weep.

"I don't get it. How can I have so many different feelings at the same time? Am I going crazy?" Confused and frightened

by his conflicting emotions, Bob struggled to hang on to the memory of Joey's first fishing pole. It had been a way to spend time with his son, even though fishing together at Lake Weslemkoon was their last time to be in each other's company.

It had only been two weeks since Joey's picture appeared in the paper celebrating his signing with the Chicago White Sox.

Unfortunately, some of their excitement became overshadowed when their pastor, Rev Rico, was arrested for molesting a child. Actually, there had been more than one and Bob was disgusted. After years of avoiding church, he had recently begun to attend at the invitation of his friend, Big Al. He liked the pastor but felt confused and betrayed by him as a man who had stood in the pulpit. Bob and Joey had talked about it on their first night at Lake Weslemkoon, trying to make sense of it all.

Joey! Reality slammed into his mind again and Bob suffered tears of rage. He couldn't stop the pain.

"Joey is gone. He's gone! My son is gone!" His thoughts screamed at him. An emotional wreck, he decided to stop in Cloyne for some lunch and some time to collect his thoughts.

* * *

Passing west of Benny's Lake on his way into town, Bob stopped at the general store and asked where he could get something to eat. It was about one o'clock in the afternoon.

The owner of the store said, "You can get a good sandwich and bowl of soup over to Sniders just up the road."

"Much obliged," Bob said.

Bob found Sniders and chose a seat near a window. The weather front had passed and he wanted to enjoy the sunlight while trying to be as invisible as possible.

A pleasant older woman in a beige apron approached the table. "What can I get ya to drink, eh?" she asked.

As Bob glanced up at her, he could tell she noticed his red rimmed eyes.

"Have you got anything stronger than beer back there?" he asked.

The waitress chuckled. "This time a day the only thing strong around here is our coffee. Made it around four this morning. Still some left. You interested?"

The thought of burnt coffee didn't seem appealing. "I'll just have ice water for now."

Bob glanced down at a fishing brochure he picked up at the Cloyne general store. *"Would fishing ever be the same?"*

The waitress put his water on the table and asked, "You ready to order?"

Bob hadn't read the menu yet, but said, "You serve eggs here?"

The waitress answered, "Yes, but they're moose eggs."

That caught Bob's attention and even brought a brief grin to his face.

"How 'bout two fried chicken eggs, bacon and some white toast?" he said. "That is, if I can still get breakfast."

"I'm taking it you want American bacon?" the waitress asked. Bob gave her a weak smile and said, "Surprise me."

He enjoyed this exchange with the waitress because it felt normal, but when his food came, he hardly tasted it. His thoughts turned to what he faced ahead; an autopsy report, a funeral and Lois.

Bob paid his bill, thanked the waitress and flung open Snider's screen door. Walking toward his car he spotted a red Ford next to it, similar to the one Big Al used to drive to the Mill. Al was a respected elder at the church and had been a good friend to Bob. Thoughts of Big Al stirred up new questions about Joey. He never had a conversation with his son about death or religion and that hit Bob hard.

"I wonder where my son is now?" he thought. *"If this religion stuff is real, I don't know if Joey is in heaven or hell!"* Bob could hardly handle the thought of his son in hell. He began to panic, needing answers.

Impulsively, Bob headed back to the restaurant and caught the attention of the waitress. "Excuse me, Ma'am, is there a library in this town?"

"Yeah, there is," she chirped. "Cloyne isn't a very big town but we do have a library and we're proud of it. We're going to be home to the North Addington Education and Training Centre next year, so we're getting a head start on a branch library of the one in Kingston, Ontario."

Too much detail for Bob. All he wanted was directions to a library.

Recognizing she went a bit over the top for the American, the waitress said, "Just keep on this road another two blocks and turn left on Little Pond Road. The library is on your left."

He turned to leave, thanking her as he went out the door.

* * *

Bob found the brick building and quickly went inside. He was on a mission, determined to find out what happens to a person after death. He knew what pastor Rico had told him, but then again, Rico lost all of his credibility with him. Bob would not rest until he found an answer.

Moving quickly past the librarian, Bob scanned the signs, looking for the religious section. It only took him a few seconds to find the aisle he needed.

There wasn't much that looked helpful but eventually he found a book called *Major Religions of the World.* That seemed like a good place to start. He found a quiet corner and began reading feverishly.

The library lights glared and the room was warm, almost too warm. Bob could feel his heart beating rapidly and sweat begin to form on his forehead, which made it tough to focus.

Taking a deep breath, he tried to slow his heartbeat. He walked to the librarian's desk and asked for a pencil and piece of paper.

Returning to his corner of the library, Bob continued his search for truth. He read, took notes, and learned a few things.

There were a lot of religions in the world and they taught many different things about how one got to heaven. Some religions taught baptism was necessary for an individual to go to heaven. Others taught that a person must stop sinning to get into heaven. Still others taught one must do good deeds, work hard and help the poor, and then hope to measure up. Some religious groups taught that God is only for them and not for all people, and others believed in multiple gods.

He read about world religions that teach reincarnation. Then he thought; *"That's one idea I won't accept! I can't imagine Joey returning as an animal or an insect. It doesn't make sense to me. In fact, none of this stuff makes sense."*

It was all pretty confusing to Bob, giving him no hope. None of it comforted his soul. How could there be so many different beliefs about life after death? How could he find out the truth? Why couldn't he find a simple answer? He just wanted to know if his son was in heaven.

Realizing he had been reading for almost an hour, Bob put the book back on the shelf and the paper in his pocket. He needed to get back on the road.

Working his way out to his car, he was no less troubled than before. *"Guess I'll have to wait to talk about this with Big Al,"* he thought. But he had hours of driving ahead with nothing but dread at the end of the road.

Once again, despair settled on Bob like a dense fog.

3

"We can't help everyone, but everyone can help someone."
Ronald Reagan

It was late when Bob pulled up next to his house in Sandusky, Ohio. Exhausted, he couldn't silence the screaming thoughts in his mind that had accompanied him all the way from Canada. What in the world was he going to say to Lois? How was he going to ease her heartache when his own heart was splintered into a thousand pieces? Pain was the story of their life now.

Distressed, he tested the conversation he would have with her at the hospital the next morning.

"Hi, Lois." That sounded so impersonal. Bob starts again.

"Lois, I got here as fast as I could! There were so many things I had to do before I left Canada..." he began, thinking it sounded weak. It was about her, he realized. Not about making excuses for himself.

Bob shook his head at the insecurity he felt, but gave it another try.

"Lois! Are you okay?" he began, trying to show concern. Bob hadn't done too well at showing concern in the past. Painfully, he remembered yelling at Lois to come help him move a picnic table in the back yard. Then he tripped over a screwdriver he had left on the ground, causing Lois to be injured. He recalled responding with anger at the inconvenience of

driving her to the hospital. Once they arrived, he discovered she was pregnant and had lost the baby.

Of course she's not ok, you idiot!" he thought to himself. *"What kind of asinine question is that? She just tried to kill herself!"*

Frustrated, Bob felt like giving up. At that moment, recognizing he was completely inadequate as a man, he desperately wished his father were alive. Even though they never had a close relationship, he knew his dad would have a no nonsense approach to a problem and not hesitate to give his opinion. But Sam Chadwick had been gone for three years.

That's when his mind went to Big Al.

*   *   *

Bob didn't sleep well his first night home. In the morning, his thoughts continued to torment him as he headed down the street to fuel up at the gas station. Once inside to pay for the gas, he got quarters to call Big Al before arriving at the hospital. As he moved toward the counter, a neighbor Bob barely knew approached him.

"Sorry to hear about your loss, Bob."

"How the hell did he hear about it already?" Bob thought to himself.

But Bob responded with his head down and a barely audible response. "Thanks," he said, as he put a quarter into the pay phone.

"Yes sir," the operator answered. "May I help you?"

"Yes, I need the number for Big Al..." Bob had forgotten Al's last name!

"We have nothing listed under the name, Big Al."

Angrily, Bob slammed the phone onto the receiver and rubbed his head. In his frustration he decided to drive over to his favorite fishing spot on the bay. It was close to his home but far away from people.

He drove back past his house and onto the back road that led to the bay. He sat down on the rock where he had spent many hours fishing and wept once again, overwhelmed by his loss. When his tears came to an end, he sat staring out over the water. It had a calming effect.

Soon, he realized, he would have to face Lois. He still had no idea what to say to her and he thought coming to this spot might help him think better. He wished he could talk with Big Al right now.

Slowly, an idea began to form. Instead of talking to Lois, maybe he should just hold her hand and let her talk if she wanted. The more he thought about it, the more he decided it was the right way to start. Bob would go from there.

4

"Listen to God with a broken heart. He is not only the doctor who mends it,
but also the father who wipes away the tears."
Criss Jami

Bob only visited hospitals five times during his adult life. The first time was when Joey entered the world. On that occasion, being at Sandusky's Providence Hospital gave reason for hope regarding the Chadwick's future as a family. Bob could imagine his son in the major leagues, wearing a New York Giants uniform.

In 1957, the Giants had moved the team to San Francisco, but in Bob's mind they would always be the *New York* Giants. He was full of dreams for his son back then. He also believed Lois would be a great mom. She would raise their boy until he was old enough. Then Bob could step in as the dad.

Bob's second visit to a hospital was five years after Joey's birth. That was the incident involving the injury to Lois and losing a baby he had no idea she was carrying. She had been fearful of his reaction if he knew and following that heartbreak, there was a strain on their marriage they never fully recovered from.

The third time Bob was in a hospital was right after his fight with Charley Somers at the steel mill. The injuries he sustained in that brawl ended his career and put him on disability for the rest of his life. Joey was fourteen years old at the time.

Two years later, Bob got the call from his mother that his dad was in the hospital and might not make it. Bob, Lois and Joey had rushed to West Virginia to see him. Although it was during that visit.

Bob's dad made amends for not being the father he should have been, it was also the last time Bob saw his father.

Today, just a few days after Joey's death at the age of eighteen, his fifth hospital visit was to his wife, in recovery after a suicide attempt. Needless to say, Bob wasn't too fond of hospitals.

*   *   *

At ten in the morning, Bob walked into Sandusky's Providence Hospital. When he asked the woman at the information desk if he could see his wife, she asked him to wait for her to contact the doctor. Fifteen minutes later, a middle-aged priest entered the waiting area.

"Mr. Chadwick, I'm Dr. Kennedy. I'm the psychiatrist on staff at the hospital. I'd like to talk with you before you see your wife."

Bob was caught off guard. Even though it was a Catholic hospital, he didn't expect his wife's doctor would be a Catholic priest. Bob didn't know whether he should call him Father or Dr. Kennedy. He settled on 'Doc.'

The doctor could see Bob's confusion over a psychiatrist wearing a priest's collar.

"Thanks for calling me 'doc," Dr. Kennedy grinned. "I like that!"

Ellison Bay 29

Bob liked Dr. Kennedy's easy manner and felt comfortable as they walked together to a conference room. He was eager to hear the doctor's assessment of his wife.

"Mr. Chadwick, first of all I want to encourage you. Lois swallowed a full bottle of sleeping pills, but someone brought her here in time to have her stomach pumped. There was no damage to internal organs. She has been sleeping quite a bit since then.

Before we discuss your wife's condition further, would you be okay if I told you more about myself?" Dr. Kennedy asked. "I don't want to bore you. However, I believe it will help you to better understand the treatment we believe will be best for Lois."

Bob smiled, appreciatively. He liked this doctor's approach and felt respected and included. He sensed he would get some direction on what to say or do when he went in to see Lois.

"Sure, Doc," he replied.

"When I began to think about psychiatry as a medical specialty in 1963," the doctor began, "I was vaguely aware of a tension between my church and the practice of psychiatry. I decided to pursue a degree in psychiatry anyway, in addition to a medical degree from Vanderbilt University.

Eventually I came to the conclusion that addressing psychiatric issues without any sense of God would be ineffective. We cannot take people apart and reassemble them without integrating the soul. It is essential to treat both. Otherwise we aren't speaking to the whole person. Even people who run away from religion cannot separate their mind from their soul. That's why I chose to work as both a psychiatrist and a priest.

"What do you mean by a *'sense of God,'* Bob ventured. He had heard similar things before but didn't know what to believe. Reading *Religions of the World* had been no help.

"Well, Mr. Chadwick..." Dr. Kennedy began.

JERRY PRICE & TOM ROY

"If you don't mind, Doc," Bob interrupted. Wanting to return the doctor's kindness he said, "Please call me Bob."

"Okay, Bob. I believe we were all built to know God and reflect his love to others. I believe God sent Jesus to show his love for us."

Already Bob understood more than he ever had. Still, he wanted to hear more.

"Bob, I'm a follower of Jesus. I believe God loved me through his Son and I believe he is the way to a relationship with the heavenly Father. My sense of God means that I don't look at people simply as physical beings with medical problems. When we eliminate God from the healing process, we are missing the mental, emotional and spiritual aspect of healing. God sees the whole person. Sometimes the greatest healing begins in the soul. Without incorporating the spiritual we are not addressing the whole person and sometimes we may do more harm than good."

"Thank you," Bob said. "I've been in hospitals before but this has me shook up more than I can explain. I appreciate your explanation about healing the soul as well as the body."

"With that in mind Bob, I'd like to help you understand what she's going through," said Dr. Kennedy.

Bob said, "That would help. Thank you."

Dr. Kennedy began to relate what happens when a person has a complete physical and emotional collapse. He was aware that their son, Joey, had died a few days earlier in Canada.

"Lois was under emotional stress, Bob," the doctor explained. "The events of the past few days overpowered her ability to cope. In my opinion, it was compounded by feelings of loneliness and rejection she has carried with her since childhood. I don't know all the details but there will be time for those conversations later. For now, my priority is to get her stabilized and resting."

Bob was listening, knowing he was likely the source of much of his wife's stress. His life had been about focusing on himself and being insensitive to her feelings.

Then he was caught off guard when he heard the doctor say, "By the way, Bob, I believe on some level you are going through many of the same things. What you have endured is more than most of us can bear alone. We are all human and here at Providence, we're here to help you both through this difficult time."

Bob wasn't quite ready to talk about his emotional unraveling. Besides, right now all he could think about was Lois getting better. However, he did want to ask Dr. Kennedy about the right approach with Lois.

"Doc, I figure about the only thing I can do when I see Lois is to hold her hand. I don't want to say something stupid. I just want her to know I'm there for her."

"That's an excellent idea, Bob!" Answered the doctor. "Take it a step at a time and after you visit with Lois, I'll be in touch with you about the treatment I believe can assist in her recovery. We'll talk about medicine that can help Lois with her feelings of being overwhelmed.

To be sure, we won't send the wrong message that she needs to 'just snap out of it.' This is going to take some time. We want to give her time to grieve the loss of her son. And we also want to bring her to a point of having a renewed sense of hope and purpose in a world that seems to be filled with nothing but pain right now."

All Bob could do was to nod his head. But in his mind he felt like the doctor was talking directly to him. He had been trying to 'snap out of it' and find answers himself for the past few days. It wasn't working for him.

* * *

It had been two months since Lois was taken to Sandusky's Providence Hospital. She went through a variety of emotions like shame, guilt, hopelessness, anxiety and loneliness, as well as the embarrassment that follows an attempt on one's life. Lois had a lot of healing to do but she gradually began to improve.

The medication helped her body to slow down and deal with the grief of losing Joey. She had individual counseling twice each week with Dr. Kennedy. They talked through her childhood, including her anger about feeling abandoned by her father at age fourteen, when he divorced her mother. After that, she had become her mom's caretaker, which forced her to grow up too fast. She had felt trapped and resented it. She grieved for her lost youth along with her grief for Joey.

She also worked through her feelings toward the His Word Community Baptist Church in Coaltown, Virginia, which held up her dad as their poster child, even though he had affairs with several women in the church. It was difficult to reconcile her feelings for the father she loved with the flawed man he had been.

Finally, she was able to tell Bob in a couple's session how she felt toward him. She resented him for being a hard and self-centered man, when what she needed was a husband she could trust to take care of her. The truth hurt.

Bob was encouraged by what the treatment was doing for Lois and how her energy was gradually returning. He understood her recovery would take time. She was still very fragile, and occasionally she would dissolve in tears with the weight of it all. They both missed Joey terribly. This was unchartered territory, trying to handle their grief together.

*   *   *

Frequently, Bob would go out to his rock; the quiet place where he could fish and think. Meanwhile, Lois would be sitting at home, lost in thought as well.

A few times in the past, Bob and Big Al had discussed what it meant to trust Jesus, but it wasn't making sense to Bob. Even though Dr. Kennedy had talked about being conscious of God in the healing process, something just didn't click for Bob. He couldn't get past feeling God had allowed all this to happen.

He was angry and decided he didn't need God. He could manage life his own way. Why not? Lois was getting better. He had been the one listening for the past several months, but what about him? As the man of the house he believed he needed to be the strong one with all the answers. But he had neither strength nor answers.

Maybe it was time to talk about what he was feeling. It would be one hell of a hard discussion.

He hoped Lois would understand. Bob stood up from his rock and headed toward his house. He knew he wanted to be careful and caring, but he would need courage for the painful discussion ahead.

As he approached the house, he took a deep breath and slowly opened the screen door. The house felt frightfully empty.

"Lois?" Bob said, softly. "Lois, where are you?"

Silence. Bob scanned the living room but it was vacant. The bedroom door was not completely closed so he gently pushed it open. No one was there. He began to get worried. Where was Lois?

"Maybe she's next door at Helen Haids' house," he thought. *"Maybe she's back in the hospital."* Uncomfortably, Bob walked into the kitchen. What should he do?

In a gesture that was all too familiar to him, he opened the fridge door and wrapped his big hand around one of his old 'buddies,' a Budweiser. He knew he should stay sober, but it seemed like old bud could offer him a little relief.

As he opened the bottle, he moved toward his comfortable chair and took a drink. The Bud tasted *so* good. Minutes later, Bob decided that his grief would be better suited with more friends in the room.

He returned to the kitchen and found several more stress relievers. After finishing his fifth beer, he fell asleep.

* * *

Lois had been visiting a neighbor because Dr. Kennedy encouraged her to find friends she trusted to talk through her pain. The person who came to mind was Ginny. They had met at Joey's school and Lois had liked her immediately. She had an easy laugh and a good listening ear. They would sit on Ginny's front porch, talking for hours.

Ginny was kind and often seemed to know just the right things to say that gave hope and perspective. Regularly, she would bring out her bible and read from the Psalms. It seemed to help. It was late and Lois knew she needed to head home.

"Thank you for letting me stay so long," she said. "Bob will be coming home soon and I should probably go."

Lois was feeling like she needed some support and comfort from her husband. Bob seemed to have changed and was treating her with more kindness than before he left with Joey for Canada. He had even hugged her a few times.

Lois waved goodbye to Ginny and walked home.

As she entered the kitchen door she sensed someone had been there. Then she noticed a muddy footprint near the fridge. She had a moment of panic, wondering if she should run. Then she heard snoring. As she walked into the living room she saw Bob surrounded by empty beer bottles.

"Not again!" she groaned, dissolving into despair. *"I wonder if there are any more of those sleeping pills..."*

5

There comes a point in your life when you realize who really matters,
who never did, and who always will.
Unknown

Finding a close friend is a gift. Most men have many acquaintances but few friends, especially the kind of friend who is safe to confide in when it comes to things that really matter. Big Al was one of those friends.

Bob and Al were sitting in a hole-in-the-wall restaurant drinking stale coffee. The place was dimly lit but Bob's relationship with Lois was even dimmer. He needed help from the only friend he could trust to tell him the truth.

*   *   *

"How do I keep screwing up so badly?" asked Bob. "I intended to come home and take care of Lois and I ended up drunk and in a deeper mess!" Al listened as Bob kept talking, noticing his conversation was mostly about himself. "My son is gone, my wife is depressed and now she's not speaking to me. I'm ready to give up!"

Big Al listened to Bob's verbal venting for several minutes before speaking.

"Welcome to life, Bob! I'm sure your intentions were good, but when things get tough, we often tend to go back to whatever makes us comfortable. You and "the buds" have been good friends for many years and although you may not want to hear this, beer is your escape. It's not really about the beer, though; it's about how you cope with life."

"I guess you're right," Bob responded after thinking about it for a few seconds, "but how did you get your life together? I wish I had half the will power you've got!"

"Hold on there, Bob." Al wanted to be careful not to give the wrong impression. "I've made plenty of mistakes in life. Like anyone else, I've made stupid decisions and caused pain for people I care about. I didn't intend to hurt anyone but the impact of my decisions affected others and I'm not proud of that.

I went to church with my family but sometimes it was just to meet girls. I'm ashamed that I was more interested in looking up their dresses than getting to know them. Sometimes the guys and I would sneak out behind the church for a cigarette and usually one of the guys brought a dirty magazine he had swiped from his dad."

This was hitting Bob a little too close to home and he began to feel uncomfortable. He wasn't sure how Al could talk so easily about his past.

* * *

"Bob, would you mind if I bring up something you said earlier?" "Sure. Go ahead."

"Okay," Al began. "You were beating yourself up about Lois coming home and finding you drunk and you said you wished you had my willpower. When I told you having a beer is how you get relief from life, you said *'I guess you're right.'* Do you remember saying that?"

Bob nodded, wondering where Al was leading.

"When you said the word *guess*, that little word tells me you haven't really bought into the idea that you escape tough times by getting drunk. I know you try hard and you don't intend to hurt other people. But the truth is your actions have hurt people, especially your wife. That's on you, my friend."

Bob was silent. He had been dealt a blow from a friend that he wasn't expecting, and it hurt. He lowered his head.

It was hard to hear, but in his heart and mind he knew it was true. Oddly, he didn't feel condemned by Al's words. In fact, he had been respected, because Al saw him as someone who could take the truth. He knew Al cared about him.

"I hear you, Al," Bob finally said.

*   *   *

Rather than pushing the issue further, Al decided to return to assuring Bob he was no different than anyone else.

"Did you know that I was drinking at a party after my high school graduation and got arrested for a DUI?" Al asked.

"*You* got arrested for a DUI!" Bob asked, disbelieving. "Yep, and I spent two nights in jail for it. After high school I started working at the mill. Drinking was a big part of my life for a while. For the first two years I spent most of my paycheck on booze and parties most weekends. I chased girls, doing more than looking up skirts, and had my own stash of girly magazines. I even had some 16mm movies! I thought I was living the life!"

"I never would have guessed!" Bob blurted out.

The hint of a smile on Bob's face was not a smirk. It was obvious Al's life had changed. Somehow hearing about his past life gave Bob a sense of hope about being able to change.

"It was after a former classmate was killed in a car accident that I began to take a serious look at my life and think what kind of man I wanted to become."

Bob could identify. Tragedy had a way of making you think that way. It was a wake-up call, for sure, but he desperately wished he could wake up and find it was all a nightmare!

"About that time, I met a race car driver named Miles," Al continued. "Because he often raced on Sundays he didn't attend church much, and some church people questioned that. But Miles was a true man of God. He told me how his life had changed when he finally understood Jesus is real and wants each of us to know Him. He had a relationship with Jesus and helped me understand I could, too. It changed my life."

Al's story was making a lot more sense to Bob than anything he had read in the book on religion.

"What was it like for you at the mill after that?" Bob asked.

"Well," Al said, remembering. "The first two years were pretty tough. The way I lived didn't change right away. The guys were always trying to trip me up and often succeeded. I used to go home at night thinking about the women they talked about. I still went to parties and hung out at the bars on weekends. There were also occasional drinking binges and one-night stands.

Even though I knew God was part of my life I didn't really know what that meant. However, as I began to read the Bible and understand it, I started making better decisions. Rather than following the crowd, I decided I would rather follow Jesus. I wanted to learn more about him."

Bob liked the way Al spoke. He was honest and never acted better than anyone else. He had always seemed like an older, wiser man to Bob, but he was slowly realizing Al had once been no better than him. Suddenly Bob was struck with a thought. *Al wasn't a better man. He was a free man.*

JERRY PRICE & TOM ROY

"We all have battles," Al was saying. "We usually don't talk about them. Maybe we're too proud to be honest and admit we don't have it all together."

"I would never have guessed you used to be so different. But come on, Al, you don't still have problems, do you? I've never seen them."

"Bob," Al laughed. "Just because I kept quiet at the mill, you think I didn't have any battles? I heard your conversations at the mill and sometimes battled ugly thoughts. There were times I hated some of you and swore at you under my breath."

"At home," he continued, "I'm embarrassed to tell you how many stupid arguments I had with my wife. I said some hateful things in anger. That's not something I wanted people to know. But that's part of the problem, Bob. I'd show up at church on Sunday and looked good on the outside to make people think I had it all together. I was all about volunteering and doing things for God. Then I ran into a wall."

"What do you mean?" Bob asked.

"The Christian life wasn't working for me. I was trying to do all the right things. I went to church, read the Bible and tried to do a good job at work. I thought if I tried to live a good life, nothing bad would happen. That's when my mom died in a car accident. Then, an uncle I looked up to, committed suicide and my girlfriend got pregnant by another guy. It felt like I had slammed into a wall."

*   *   *

In a flash he saw the fight at the mill, his injury and early retirement, Joey's death and Lois trying to kill herself. Life had brought Bob to a dead stop as well, and he didn't know how to push through. But if the Christian life wasn't working for Al, what hope was there for him?

Al broke into his thoughts. "Life was not working out like I thought it should. I had to have a long talk with Jesus, and that talk lasted almost three months! I thought it was all about me living a good life. I thought if I did my share of good deeds, God owed me a good life! But Jesus showed me it wasn't about me at all.

I drank a lot during those months. Honestly, it was hell. I began to see that I was full of selfishness and pride. I thought I could do it all myself. When I couldn't, I felt like a failure. I began to understand that Jesus wants to partner with us. He wants me to trust *him* to change me into the person he created me to be. He never promised us a life without struggle, but he promised to give us wisdom and comfort in whatever we are going through.

I realized I had been thinking only about myself. Jesus changed my focus and showed me I needed to think more about others and how my actions affect them."

Bob began to feel uncomfortable again. Guilty! He had a habit of thinking only about himself.

"Believe me, Bob, I do have problems and some of those problems I only discuss with Jesus! I battle with the same things as any other man. I may seem like a pretty good guy now, but honestly I would rather be seen simply as someone who loves Jesus."

"Wow Al, I always thought you were perfect," Bob responded, smiling. Both men laughed.

"Far from it," Al said, shaking his head. "When you met me I was beginning to mature in my faith, but I was afraid to talk about it at the mill. Those guys can be a pretty tough group, as you know. But I'm so glad you decided to show up at the church."

* * *

It felt good to talk with Al. It took Bob's mind off his own problems for a while.

"Yeah, about church." Bob took a breath. "Sometime I want to talk with you about that. I can't seem to get over what Pastor Rico did. But right now I need to focus on Lois. What should I do, Al? How do I get out of this mess I'm in?"

"Well, buddy, do you really want to hear what I have to say?" Bob knew that he would probably have to swallow his pride again and ask for forgiveness. But how many times would Lois buy it? Cautiously curious, Bob said, "Sure do Bob. Go for it."

"Ok. As you know, Lois is very fragile right now. Not only is she dealing with the loss of a son, but a husband who is passed out drunk when she needs him most. I wouldn't be surprised if she is contemplating taking her life again. How was she acting when you left the house?"

Bob looked down at his hands. "I couldn't sleep last night. About four this morning I went outside and just sat in the car. I wasn't even there when she woke up."

That news jolted Al. "We need to get back to your house as soon as possible! Lois may despise you right now but she needs you!"

Bob got up to pay for the coffee while Al went out to start the car.

"I'll drive," Al said as he went out the door. We can pick up your car later." Bob didn't protest.

* * *

As they sped toward Bob's house, both men silently speculated on the scene they might find. The door was locked when they arrived. Bob took out his keys and they walked into a silent house. There was a half full pot of coffee and an empty cup on the counter.

With a pit in his stomach, Al asked, "Where's the bedroom?"

Al hurried in the direction Bob pointed and as he turned the corner he saw Lois standing in the bathroom with a bottle of pills in her hand.

"Lois, please don't!" Al shouted.

Lois was startled and dropped the bottle. When she saw Al, she crumpled into a heap on the floor, covering her head in shame. He noticed the bottle of pills on the floor. It was almost full. *Good*, he thought, hoping they were not too late.

Gently, Al placed a hand on her shoulder. "When you're ready, I'd like to talk with you."

Lois sat motionless while Al waited patiently. Finally, he asked how many pills she had taken. She remained silent.

"Lois, how many pills did you take?"

"I didn't take any yet. I just want some peace." He could hardly hear her.

Al was relieved. "Lois, God has something for you in life. I am so glad you didn't do something foolish."

"God?" Her voice grew louder. "Where was God when Joey died? Where was he when Bob made me lose my baby girl? Or when he treats me like I'm nothing but trash? Don't talk to me about God!"

When Al helped her to stand up, Lois noticed Bob standing in the hallway. All he got was a cold stare and slowly, he backed down the hall.

Al was deeply concerned for Lois but also encouraged by how she was able to express her anger. To him, it seemed like a good thing.

He quickly shot up a silent prayer and then said, "Lois, I think it would be a good idea to talk with your doctor. Are you willing to do that?"

She was not.

"You think I am nuts, don't you?" Lois defensively asked.

"No, I don't think that at all. I think you've been through some terrible things and you need help processing all that has happened, including what Bob did last night."

It took some convincing and finally Lois agreed to go, but only if Bob wasn't going. In agreement, Bob nods his head and Al slowly walked Lois out to his car. Before he left, Al said, "Oh, and Bob? Stay away from your *buddies*!"

"Yes, sir," Bob responded; like a soldier saluting an officer.

* * *

When they arrived at the hospital Al was surprised Dr. Kick had an opening in his schedule to see Lois. He invited her into his office as Al settled himself in the lobby with a *Time* magazine.

* * *

Back at the house, Bob seemed lost. *What am I going to do?* He asked himself. *Go fishing?*"

But his recent memory of fishing with Joey canceled out that interest. Before settling down to watch some daytime TV,

Bob walked to the kitchen and opened the fridge. Once again he felt the powerful desire for *his buds*.

"No way!" he shouted out loud and made his way back to the living room.

6

Too often we underestimate the power of a touch, a smile, a kind
word, a listening ear, an honest compliment, or the
smallest act of caring, all of which have the potential to
turn a life around.
Leo Buscaglia

"Ladies and gentlemen, I introduce to you the graduating
class of 1973!"

Bob was thinking about the moment just months earlier when Joey had graduated with such a bright future. Now he was left with only the *'what ifs'* of his life.

His mind eventually drifted back to the question that had haunted him on his drive home from Canada.

"Where is Joey now? Is there really life after death? Is this life worth living?

Maybe Lois has the right idea.

Then he heard the phone ring. He moved quickly from his chair into the kitchen and answered the call.

"Hello."

"Bob, this is Al. They are going to keep Lois in the hospital for a night or two. I just wanted you to know. I'll come to get you in thirty minutes and we can pick up your car."

"Okay Al. Sounds like a plan."

*   *   *

As Bob hung up the phone, the cord caught on the handle of the coffee pot, spilling coffee all over the floor. "Damn that coffee pot," he blurted out!

Instantly the memory returned of Joey as an infant being burned by coffee he had spilled on him.

"Man, every time I turn around, there are reminders of my son and what a *putz* I am!"

In the past, Bob's tendency was to minimize his behavior or blame someone else for it. This time he caught himself doing the same thing by only calling himself a *putz*.

The truth? He was worse than a putz!

Bob had been hung over after celebrating the Giants third game World Series win. The next morning he stumbled into the kitchen, in need of coffee. After pouring himself a cup, he turned toward the table and caught his foot on the playpen, splashing steaming coffee down Joey's face and the right side of his body.

"Joey!" Lois had shrieked, as she grabbed her son and rushed to the sink to run cool water over the skin where the coffee had badly scalded him.

"You shouldn't have put the playpen in the kitchen!" Bob had hollered at Lois.

But, his son's screaming drowned out Bob's yelling.

Joey cried all the way to the emergency room. Lois was crying silently and Bob was muttering under his breath, "I hope this doesn't ruin his chance to play in the big leagues!"

"I'm much worse than a putz," Bob thought. *"I'm an arrogant, narrow-minded, self-centered bastard! I've been drunk or hung over most of my life and I've refused to be honest about the kind of man I've been."*

After cleaning up the spilled coffee, Bob shuffled back to his chair, muttering, *"Here I am home alone again. This really sucks!"*

JERRY PRICE & TOM ROY

What Bob was really thinking was, *"Can I handle life alone without my buds?"* He seriously doubted that he could do it. So he decided to make a personal pact and swore *not to drink*. He knew in his heart the pact was about as solid as a political promise, but it made him feel better for the moment.

Just as he was promising himself not to take another drink, Al showed up in the driveway.

"How's she doing, Al?" Bob asked.

Pointedly, Al said, "I think Lois will be fine Bob, but she needs some reassurance and encouragement to get through this."

"OK, thanks for everything, Al." Bob said, avoiding Al's gaze. "You're a godsend."

Al went along with him but shot back, "Well Bob, thanks for acknowledging God!"

They both chuckled a bit.

After an uncomfortable silence, Bob blurted out, "Al, I was wondering if you would mind if I stayed the next two nights with you? I just don't trust myself alone here."

Al thought for a second and responded, "I think that will work. Where's your phone, Bob? My brother is staying with me right now and I want to ask him if he minds having another house guest."

"It's over there by the counter," Bob replied.

Al moved that way and almost lost his balanced while slipping on a wet floor.

"Sorry about that Al, I had a little accident. You ok?"

"Yeah, I am fine," but he seemed perturbed Bob hadn't warned him about the wet floor. At his age he was always conscious of what a fall could do to him.

Al picked up the phone and made his call. His brother was agreeable so Bob packed a few essentials and went with Al to pick up his car and follow him to the house.

*   *   *

Al's younger brother, Richard, was waiting for them. He was a pleasant man in his mid-sixties with graying hair and stylish clothes.

"Bob, let me introduce you to my brother, Richard."

"Hey, Richard, how're you doing? Thanks for letting me stay with you guys."

"No problem, Bob. There's an extra bedroom. But really, how are *you* doing? You and your wife have had a tough time lately."

If he only knew! Bob didn't answer but thanked him for asking as they walked into the house.

Al's house was much like the one Lois and Bob lived in, with a few upgrades. It was a fifties ranch with a basement and detached garage.

"Let me show you your room, Bob," Richard offered.

The bedroom was simple but comfortable. There was a dresser, a nightstand and a double bed that looked inviting.

"The bathroom is down the hall and the gray towels are yours. We only have the one bathroom, but we can make it work."
"I'll work around your schedules," Bob offered.

"Well, we don't have much of a schedule for the next few days, so let's just see how things work out. Hope you feel welcome, Bob."

"I appreciate it," he answered.

"Glad to help out. I'll look forward to getting to know you better," Richard said, with a backward glance.

Bob unpacked his small duffle bag. As he walked back toward the living room, he realized he had no idea how to unpack the mess he made of his life.

*   *   *

Al had already put on a pot of coffee and was ready for Bob when he came out of his room. Richard wasn't around. Bob figured he must have gone out for the evening.

"All unpacked, friend?"

"Yep. Don't need much for a couple of nights."

"I hope you're comfortable. Make yourself at home. If you need something and you don't see it, just ask."

"Thanks, Al."

There was a pause before Al spoke. "Well Bob," he said thoughtfully, "we have some things to talk about. Your wife is not doing well."

"I know," Bob said, lowering his head. "I've never seen her like this."

Bob was uncomfortable. His instinct was to avoid uncomfortable situations but he knew Al wasn't going to let him off the hook.

"What Lois is going through is more than grieving for her son. When Lois found you passed out drunk, it brought back memories of all the other times you've treated her badly, Bob."

BOOM! Al was diving right in! Bob tried to hide the discomfort, but his face looked like he had been punched in the gut.

Al knew Bob didn't want to talk about it, but he cared deeply for them. And, clearly, he wasn't worrying about making Bob uncomfortable.

"Fortunately, she has excellent care, but she's got a long way to go. You're going to have to give her some time to get back to normal; whatever that looks like. You two have been through some tough stuff, especially with losing Joey. But Lois is dealing with more than grief. Sometimes a crisis has a way of exposing other things."

Bob didn't know what to say. He simply shook his head.

You will need to come up with an intentional way to navigate the first few days together, Bob. But even if you make up, the real issue is much deeper than appeasing your wife. You need to deal with your own issues. You have a habit of defaulting to selfishness and anger."

Ouch! Bob couldn't argue with Al about that one.

"I know that sounds harsh," Al said, "and you might be upset with me. That's OK, but will you give it some honest thought? I'll leave you alone for a while so you can think through some things."

Bob was caught off guard. It seemed pretty abrupt, but he responded, without much emotion, "Whatever you think is best Al."

* * *

Bob took his coffee back to his room and locked the door. He sat down on the bed with no idea of what he was supposed to think about. He was much more comfortable with hard work than hard thinking.

Gradually his thoughts wandered back to West Virginia. His childhood, plainly, was less than ideal. His father was an adulterer and an abuser. His mother never said much.

He remembered feeling lonely and sitting in his room for days, doing nothing. He didn't like his home, his family or his life. Bob cut into his own thoughts, telling himself to think about more pleasant memories.

He remembered a few family picnics. He remembered the smell of home baked bread and how he loved sneaking cookies from the cookie jar without getting caught. He remembered his dad occasionally taking him fishing down at the river. Sometimes there were school outings and one time he had gone to a stock car race.

Although he was voted most likely to succeed in his senior class of twenty-five, for the most part Bob barely tolerated school.

Truthfully, he never thought he needed an education. He just wanted to get a job, buy a car, and move out of the house.

Bob stared out the window, trying to come up with more pleasant memories, but nothing came to mind. His entire childhood seemed to be covered by some enormous, oppressive cloud of sadness.

Sadness was an unfamiliar emotion for Bob. Oddly, Bob noticed that none of these memories evoked anger. Normally he reverted to anger. He sat still for a moment, and for the first time in his life allowed himself to feel the sadness of his childhood. Somehow, the feeling seemed right and more memories began to flood his mind.

He remembered the Friday nights when his dad would get drunk on a $1.50 bottle of Kaczmarek Vodka. He could picture him in his chair, complaining or barking orders. There were no conversations in the house; just his dad making sure he was heard.

He remembered his mom, looking timid and disheveled, waiting on his dad.

There was the time he saw his dad beat his mother, and he had watched, terrified and helpless. That was the time he vowed never to cry again. He began to feel empty on the inside but tried to cover it up by staying hard on the outside.

As he thought about his childhood, Bob began to wonder why he didn't have more memories. What about the time between graduating and meeting Lois? He had gone to work in the mines after high school. Why were those years such a blank?

Was it because he hated working in the mines? Was it because of the arguments with his father about wanting to get out of the mines? Was it because of the time one of the older miners had accosted him?

Wait! Where did that come from? Bob had forgotten about that!

*   *   *

The oppressive cloud of sadness over Bob turned dark and angry. He felt a rage rising within that terrified him. As details began to reveal themselves in his memory, they unlocked more savage rage, and Bob knew that if he hadn't been in Al's home he would have destroyed something or someone. He wanted to scream out his pain.

Bob had been young to work in the mines, but got the go ahead because of his dad's reputation. One day he had taken a break when one of the older miners—a big, burly man—came into the men's room and pushed Bob into the urinal while he was relieving himself.

"You need tweezers to grab that thing, kid?"

Roughly, the man yanked Bob away from the stall, making him pee all over the floor.

The man laughed out loud and exclaimed, "Well, you do have a dick!" Bob froze, mortified.

"Drop those drawers, kid, and show me your goods!" Bob felt paralyzed. The man jerked down his jeans.

"Nice little twig 'n berries, kid," the man said, pushing his face close to Bob. The man reeked of sweat and filth. "You ever use that thing for anything other than pissin?"

Bob was aware of his arm hurting from the man's grip, when suddenly the man reached down with his other hand and touched him!

Bob's mind went blank. He imagined himself alone in a boat, fishing. At least his mind could be in an imaginary safe place while his body was being molested!

He knew he couldn't physically overcome the man. There was no escape, so whatever happened, happened. When it was over, Bob remembered hearing the man say, "From now on, I'm gonna call you peewee. This is *our* little secret, kid. Keep it that way!" the man berated. In shock, Bob cowered in the corner. He didn't remember how long.

Pulling up his pants, he finally ran out of the restroom and returned to work. He had no idea how much the other miners knew. But the name stuck.

Bob was convulsed with the pain of this memory.

*   *   *

None of Bob's memories of working in the mine were pleasant, including the argument with his dad. He and Lois were married at the time and he had expressed his wish to get a job outside of the mine.

In front of Lois his dad had declared that 'real men' work in the mines. Bob felt the old resentment rising in him. In his mind Sam Chadwick had no idea what a real man was.

"You think you know what a 'real man' is?" Bob shouted silently at his dad. *"You didn't see what that pervert did to me.*

You weren't there! In fact, you weren't there for most of my life!"

It wasn't long after that argument that Bob and Lois left for Sandusky Bay and a new life. Thinking back to those days, Bob came to a conclusion. *It was much easier to be angry than to feel sad.*

Somehow anger felt good to Bob. It gave him a sense of control that he had never possessed with all the sadness he had known. He had grown up in a home that wasn't safe and no one was protected, no one except his dad.

* * *

"Enough of this!" Bob thought. He turned to thinking about his marriage, remembering his wedding day and the first few months of married life. He smiled thinly, recalling a few happy times.

He also recalled the anger he brought home from the mill every day. Shortly after that argument with his dad, he and Lois had moved to Sandusky where he began working at the steel mill.

More recent memories flashed through Bob's mind like a silent film, some pleasant and some painful. *The day Joey was born, fishing with Joey, catching Joey looking at his stash of porn, the fight at the mill, meeting Reverend Rico, visiting his church and conversations with Al.*

He tried to sort it all out and make some sense of his life, but nothing seemed to make sense.

"I don't understand why I act like I do!" Bob thought. But he had a hunch the memories that had flashed through his mind were unlocking something inside him.

Though he fought it, the recent memory of Joey's death and the agony of the week that followed pushed itself into Bob's thoughts. The drive home and the funeral arrangements were a blur. But one incident stood out to him.

There was a line out the door of the funeral home the day of the viewing. Friends of Joey's from the high school, coaches, some of Bob's coworkers from the mill and even a few old acquaintances from Coaltown showed up.

Bob was greeting a couple of the visitors from Coaltown he had known from the mine. Fortunately, they didn't call him *Peewee!* As he was shaking hands with one of them, he noticed the other one didn't let go right away when he shook Lois' hand, and he winked at her when he did.

That didn't sit right with Bob. Lois blushed and lowered her head. Bob hadn't given it much thought at the time, but now it began to bother him.

"Enough of this!" Bob thought.

He had spent less than half an hour in thought but it seemed like days. He opened the door and went looking for Al.

*   *   *

"Well, Bob, that was short!"

"Not much of a life, I guess," Bob shrugged. Truthfully, Bob thought much of his life had flashed in front of him and he didn't like most of what he saw. He didn't like facing the sadness he had known. He didn't like feeling weak and helpless. He had reverted to anger as a wall to block it out. He was stunned to realize Lois had no idea about many things in his life.

Al poured another cup of coffee. "Well buddy, tell me what you learned."

Bob poured out his story. When he was finished, Al spoke quietly, "I know this isn't easy to talk about. Do you mind if I dig a little deeper?"

Bob trusted Al. He knew what they talked about would stay between them. And he knew Al would help him figure things out.

"Go ahead, Al."

One event stuck out to Al.

"When you were in the restroom in the mine, how did you feel?" Al asked.

Bob lowered his head in shame.

"That was a huge moment in your life, Bob, and it framed how you view yourself. I think it was at that point you decided to make sure you would always be in charge and never let anyone hurt you again. And that, my friend, has damaged you."

Bob was listening.

"It's a good thing to talk about stuff like this, Bob, and it helps to begin figuring things out. But it's only a start." Al paused to let Bob absorb this.

Are you open to another question?" "I'll give it a shot, Al."

"Have you ever wept for that young kid who was sexually abused?"

7

*"If you had started doing anything two weeks ago, by today you would
have been two weeks better at it."*
John Mayer

The next morning Bob was awakened by the radio alarm
playing a song by the Byrds. *"I was much older than that then; I
am younger than that now."* It was strange to hear that song
right then. Bob remembered singing along to the Byrds on the car
radio on his way to work, but he had never understood the
meaning of the lyrics.

Al, like an old sage, had challenged Bob to think about why
he had become such an angry, abusive man. Thinking back
through events in his early years had helped him begin to put a
few pieces together. During his working years he had thrown
himself into his job and had been unavailable to his wife and son.
Al would call him *'emotionally and relationally constipated.'*

Bob now realized there was a link between his past and his
present behavior. And with that, he became motivated to
understand more and make some meaningful changes.

Al was already in the kitchen when Bob walked in.

"Morning, Bob. Coffee?"

"Please." Bob nodded.

Al was aware how their conversation the day before
plowed up some pain and realized Bob may have had a rough
night. He knew Bob didn't realize it yet, but the purpose for
digging into the past wasn't to find someone to blame and

become a 'victim,' giving himself permission to be a jerk. The purpose was to find out when he started acquiring harmful thinking patterns; learning along the way to manipulate people to keep them off his back. Then, to compensate for his loneliness, he had developed a relationship with his *'buds.'*

"Thought I'd cook us Breakfast. How do you like your eggs?"

"Over easy," Bob answered. "Thanks for cooking. And thanks for talking last night, even though it was tough. It took me a while to get to sleep."

Al appreciated the word of thanks, but he noticed Bob's unwitting insistence to put the focus on his self. Yes, this was a painful time for him, but Al hoped it would give Bob an opportunity to grow as a man and learn how to love others.

"Grab a plate and come get your eggs. There's toast in the toaster. Anything else you need?"

"Do you have any orange juice?" Bob asked. "Sure do. It's in the fridge."

Bob got the juice and made his way to the table. "I owe you for all of this, Al. I owe you a favor."

"You owe me?" Al stopped cooking and gave Bob a hard look. "I don't play that game."

"Game?" Bob thought. He was a bit put off by Al's touchiness. This was the first time he'd had a reaction like that but decided to let it go.

After working together at the mill and getting to know Bob personally, Al was aware that he had a way of obligating others to himself by playing the *'I owe you'* game. It was very difficult for Bob to accept kindness from anyone unless he could pay back the favor.

* * *

When Al's toast popped up he carried his plate to the table and offered a prayer.

"Thank you, Father, for this food and for another day of life. We are grateful for health and we hope you will be honored in our lives. We pray for Lois today and ask you to heal her heartache. We ask this in Jesus' name. Amen."

Bob wondered why Al's prayers seemed so real. He and Lois hardly ever prayed together. In fact, the only time was when Lois occasionally recited a prayer before a meal. There was something different about how Al prayed.

"Al, you talk to God like he's your friend."

"Thanks, Bob. He is! In fact, I see him as more than a friend.

He's the Creator of the universe and I'm awed to think he would care about listening to me." Al said. "Tell me about how you pray?"

Bob was caught off guard by the question and answered with a wry smile. "Well, I guess I don't pray much unless I'm in trouble or I want something." As he was speaking, Bob could hear his own selfishness in what he said.

"Each morning I try to read something from the Bible. It helps me gain perspective for the day ahead." Al ventured. "Do you mind if I read it out loud?"

"Fine with me," Bob answered.

Al reached for his bible and began to turn the pages. "I was just about to begin reading the first chapter of 1 Peter."

*   *   *

It took less than five minutes to read the chapter, but Bob got lost in the forest of words.

Reading the look on Bob's face, Al said, "There's a lot of good stuff in there! Would you like me to break it down a bit?"

"Sure," Bob replied somewhat halfheartedly.

"Peter is writing to people who had scattered because of persecution and needed hope. I guess we're all there at times, right?"

"I get that part," Bob answered. "Right now I'm feeling scattered in the head!"

As Al scanned the page, words like *elect, sanctification, obedience, blood, grace and mercy* jumped out at him.

"Did you understand any of what this chapter is about?"
"Not really, but I'm listening."

"Ok, let's talk about a few words at the beginning of the chapter. The word *elect* is talking about how God chose us. He *elected* to have a relationship with us. We don't deserve it, but God loves us and wants us to know him.

The word *sanctification* is the process of figuring out what that relationship is supposed to look like.

The word *obedience* talks about having a heart to follow God. It doesn't mean we will be perfect, but God wants us to trust him.

The word *blood* is powerful. Most people think they have to be good enough to have a relationship with God. That's impossible and it's actually an insult to God. There is no way we can be good enough. It was Jesus' death that makes it possible for us to have a relationship with God. The blood he shed when he gave his life is the only thing that can cover our sin.

Grace is a word that describes the gift God gave us when he made a way for us to know him. Grace is kindness we don't deserve.

Mercy is what forgiveness looks like. When we make a mess of our lives because of our selfishness, we deserve judgment. Instead, he offers us a pardon."

Bob was beginning to feel overwhelmed! He had attended church a few times and understood part of what Al was saying. He was drawn to Al's passion and wished he had some of that emotion. But it felt like he was drinking from a fire hose. Much of what Al said flooded past his limited understanding of God.

"Were there any words in this chapter that caught your attention?" Al broke into Bob's thoughts.

"*Grief* and *trials*," Bob said, with a bitter half-smile. "That kind of says it all about my life."

Al began to explain that the Christian life is not easy or problem free.

"With Jesus we gain a different perspective on our grief and troubles. Our problems, though real, are temporary. Eventually, the pain of losing your son will ease, but it won't ever completely go away in this life. But Jesus said there's going to be a day when he'll wipe all our tears away.

It's tempting to feel like a victim when life gets tough, but the truth is our trials give us an opportunity to trust God and grow in our faith. In a way, hard times can be a gift if they move us toward seeking God."

"I don't know, Al." Bob said. "I guess I'm not there yet. With everything that's happened to me in the past few months, it's hard to think about all this."

"*Happened to you?*" Bob interrupted. "Are you forgetting you have a wife who's had plenty of grief and trials herself, including you?"

That hit hard. It was a reality slap that brought Bob's current situation into sharp focus. He'd thought about himself and his own problems when Lois, his wife, was suffering more deeply than him.

Bob was beginning to understand where Al was leading in their conversations. He knew Al for sixteen years and believed in his heart Al honestly cared about him. Although he understood he was guilty, he also knew Al wasn't condemning him. He simply didn't mince words with him or treat him like a baby. In fact, he felt Al respected him enough to be straightforward and honest.

* * *

"What do you think we should do about Lois?" Bob asked, his thoughts shifting to his wife.

"I don't think there's much we can other than give her time. I could call the center and see how she's doing." Al responded.

"That would be great. Will you? I understand I've been self centered in thinking about myself but I do care about her," Bob said, feeling some remorse.

"Sure, I can do that."

When the secretary answered the phone she was able to let Al know that Lois was doing a little better. She said the doctor was scheduled to be in later that afternoon and she would be glad to have him give Al a call.

"Wonderful. Thank you," Al said.

Al was relaying the message to Bob when Richard wandered into the kitchen in his bathrobe. "Sorry I slept so late," Richard said, "but it sure felt good!"

"No problem," Bob answered, "we've just been enjoying breakfast and good conversation."

"Got any left?" Richard asked, as he poured himself a cup of coffee. "I'm hungry!"

"Eggs are in the fridge," Al answered to spoil Richard's hope that he would cook his brother's breakfast.

"What are you guys doing today?" Richard asked, cracking two eggs into the skillet. "Remember that pile of junk out back? You were going to take it to the dump." Richard had helped Al clean out years of accumulation in the basement and garage.

Bob jumped at the suggestion. "I'd be glad to help," he offered. He'd had enough Bible lessons for a while.

"Ok," Al agreed. They threw on some old clothes while Richard finished his breakfast and met in the back yard.

* * *

The two men loaded Al's old Chevy pickup and chatted on the way to the dump about how easy it was to accumulate junk. After paying a small fee, they unloaded and climbed back into the truck. Down the road, Bob asked about Al's brother.

"Richard was married a little more than a year," Al began. "Let's just say he decided he didn't like women."

That ended the discussion.

"Let's get cleaned up and I'll take you out for lunch. There's a little hole-in-the-wall place just outside of town that has great burgers." Al offered.

"Sounds good, but I'm buying." Bob responded. To his surprise, Al didn't argue.

8

"Anger is the most impotent of passions. It effects nothing it goes about, and hurts the one who is possessed by it more than the one against whom it is directed."
Carl Sandburg

Al pulled open the rusted screen door, hanging crooked on its hinges. Mo's was located in a cement block building with a faded sign that said, *Mo's Custom Meats*. As the men walked in, Bob almost tripped over an old hound dog lying on a rug covering part of the concrete floor.

"Anyone home?" Al called out.

"Sit down!" shouted a rough voice from behind a swinging door. "I'll be right out!"

"You'll enjoy meeting Mo. He's an interesting guy," Al told Bob, nodding toward a scarred wooden table with four metal chairs in the corner.

As Bob was taking in the faded green paint, the sparse furnishings and the menu scrawled on a chalkboard, Mo walked out of the kitchen, wearing a white butcher's coat and a ready smile. He was a big man with broad shoulders and a barrel chest. Wiping his hands on the already bloodstained jacket, he reached out to shake Al's hand.

Noticing Bob's expression, he said, "What's the matter, buddy? You've never seen a butcher before?"

Al laughed out loud. "Mo, meet my friend, Bob."

"I'll shake your hand if you're not afraid of a little blood," Mo said with a smile. Bob liked this guy's style. He had a refreshing blend of humor and honesty.

"Thought I'd introduce Bob to your great burgers, Mo," Al began, "but I was also hoping you'd have time to sit down and visit. Got a few minutes?"

"What the hell do you think this is?" Mo had a twinkle in his eyes. "I'm trying to make a living and you want me to sit around and chew the fat?"

"Exactly," Al fired back, looking pointedly at the empty room, grinning.

Mo cracked a small smile. "I knew you'd say that. Today's a slow day. Let me go wash my hands and I'll be right back."

As Mo was cleaning up, Al gave Bob a little background.

"Mo and his wife bought this place about ten years ago. They wanted to make it different from other restaurants in the area. Mo grew up in his family's butcher shop back in New York so they decided he would butcher their own meat. They buy from local farmers and all the meat they serve is butchered here. They also butcher meat to order."

"Makes sense to me," Bob said. "I like this place."

"His real name is Massimo. Mo for short. He and his wife, Linda, visited Cedar Point and fell in love with the area. The restaurant was for sale and they decided to take a chance. They kept the restaurant 'casual,' as you can see, and the locals loved it. Mo came from a rough background," Al continued. "He got involved with drugs which led to other crimes. He spent more than a few nights in jail. He was thirty-five when he got his life straightened out and moved to Sandusky."

Mo reappeared wearing a clean apron. "You guys want anything to drink?"

"Coke and a burger for me," Al answered.

"I didn't ask what you wanted to eat!" Mo said, before Bob could add his order. "Cokes for both of us," Al said, chuckling.

Placing two cold colas in front of them, Mo said, "So, you guys want to eat or talk? Make up your minds!"

"Both," said Al, laughing again. "Let's talk first and then we'll take those burgers."

Throwing down a couple of straws, Mo took a seat. "Welcome to Mo's, *Bawb*."

"It's Bob," Al corrected.

"Maybe to you, but in New *Yawk*, he's *Bawb*!" Mo had a hearty laugh.

*   *   *

"Bob lost his son in an accident in Canada just a few months ago," Al began, "and his wife is in the hospital. I wanted him to meet you."

"Whoa! Way to start out light and build up to heavy!" Mo placed a beefy hand on Bob's shoulder. "Sorry to hear that."

"Bob's staying at my house for a few days. I thought he needed a dose of Mo's reality along with a Mo's burger."

"I'll do my best." Mo answered. "By the way, refills are free on the cokes, but the burgers will cost ya a buck-twenty five each. Cash only."

"I really like this guy," Bob thought, taking a long sip of his coke.

"Would you mind giving us the *Reader's Digest* version of the past ten years?" Al asked Mo.

"Sure. My wife and I moved here a while ago and bought this place. It took a while to make a go of it, but the locals supported us and after a couple years we were doing pretty well."

Mo's voice softened as he continued. "Linda got pregnant with our first child and Suzanne was born later that year. Everything was going fine until…" Mo's voice grew huskier.

"Until one day when Linda was closing up alone. I had cleaned up the back and taken Suzanne home. When it got late I got worried and called the cops. They found the place unlocked and the cash register empty. It took 'em a couple weeks but they found her body in a wooded area about thirty miles south. She'd been raped and stabbed. They never found the guy.

With that, Mo got up and walked over to the grill behind the counter. "How do you want those burgers?" he asked.

Bob was stunned. He couldn't imagine anyone having it worse than he did, but Mo's story left him speechless.

"The usual for me," Al said. "Just mustard and ketchup." "Same for me," Bob said. "And fried onions, if you have them."

Looking at Al, he said in a low voice, "Is this for real?"

"Yeah, I'm afraid it is." Al nodded. "I've been meeting with him for the past few years. The other day I told Mo it would be a good idea for him to share his story with someone else. I thought you needed to hear what he had to say."

"We've been studying the bible together here every Tuesday morning before he opens." Al continued. "He's come a long way. He turned his life over to Christ about a year ago. He's still rough around the edges, but he knows without a doubt that God loves him. He's at a place where he wants to help others. Today was the start."

Mo brought two baskets with burgers and fries over to the table and sat back down. "How did I do, boss?" he asked, with a wide smile.

"I'm proud of you, my friend!" Al answered. "You took a chance."

Bob couldn't get over Mo's story. "I'm so sorry for what happened," he said.

"Thanks." Mo's voice grew husky again. "Nothing I can do about the past. It hurts every time I think about it, but life goes on. I have to admit, though, it's tough every time a new guy comes through that door. I'm suspicious of their motives."

"I can imagine," Bob said, taking a bite of his burger. "Not much else to say, I guess." Mo shrugged.

Al thought differently. "Why don't you tell Bob how you put your faith in Jesus and how that's affected you?"

*　*　*

"Sure," Mo said. "This big jerk used to come in a couple of times a week. One day I was being my usual sarcastic self and he asked me why I was such a hard ass, or something like that," he said, elbowing Al. "He said, *'I bet there's a nice guy inside there somewhere.'* I told him I was just a piece of shit and always would be. He didn't preach at me. He just looked at me and kept showing up."

"Sometimes, if business was slow, I'd sit down and we'd talk. You know, just small talk. He'd ask about the restaurant business. Once he even offered to help and I told him to keep the hell out of my business 'cuz he'd screw it up! He never seemed bothered by my crudeness and like I said, he just kept coming back."

"Then one day while he was sitting at the counter he asked about my family. He had no idea he'd hit on such a sore spot. I threw down my spatula and walked out of the room. When I returned Al never mentioned it again."

"About a month later he was here eating lunch and Suzanne walked out from the back room. She was just a little thing but she had a big personality, like her mama. She went right over to Al and sat down beside him. I heard her telling him, *'I wish I had my mama.'* I grabbed her hand and told her to stay in the back room."

"Al came one day as the lunch crowd was thinning out and he asked me if I felt like talking. I guess I was ready. We sat for two hours and he listened while I poured out my story. When I was finished he gave me a huge hug. That was a first for me," Mo said, punching Al in the shoulder, "but I needed it."

"We developed a friendship and I started to trust him. He not only helped me navigate through a truckload of pain, he talked to me about Jesus. It started to make sense to me. I'd screwed up a lot in my life and Jesus suffered for me. It took about two years, but I finally turned my life over to him. Believing in Jesus wasn't too hard for me but giving up control was. Eventually, I decided he could do a better job than I had!"

"Then the really tough part came. As Al and I met and I began to understand the Bible, I realized Jesus was asking me to forgive. I knew he had forgiven me, but forgiving the creep that killed my wife? That wasn't going to happen!"

"I struggled with this for a long time before I realized the guy who killed my wife probably wasn't thinking much about what he did, but I was. It was like I was taking the poison and hoping he would die! By the way, they never found him. For all I know, he's still out there. About six months ago, after Al helped me understand forgiveness, I decided not to hold a grudge against the guy.

There are still times I fantasize about killing the guy, but I have to remember that forgiving this criminal doesn't mean forgetting what happened. It means I give up my right to get even with him and let God take care of that business."

JERRY PRICE & TOM ROY

Just then, a cute little girl walked in the back door. "Hey, Suzy, look who's here. It's 'Uncle Al' and he's brought us a new friend. This is Bob."

Suzanne ran over to Al and hugged him. "Hi, Bob. Hi, Uncle Al," she said.

Al chuckled as he embraced the little girl. "What did you learn in school today?" he asked.

"Well, third grade is a *lot* harder than second grade!" she said. Al laughed.

"We get new vocabulary words every week and I'm the best speller in my class."

"Wow, that's impressive. I bet your dad is proud of you!" Al exclaimed.

"You bet I am," Mo said, "but right now you need to go back and work on your vocabulary words. You don't want to let someone else take the top spot, do you?"

With that Suzanne scampered into the back room.

"What a sweet girl," Bob observed, watching her skip away. "Yeah, pretty amazing, isn't it, considering she's got me for a dad?" Mo laughed easily. "Good thing she's got a lot of her mother in her."

Bob was sobered just thinking about all these two had survived. "Well, Bob and I should get moving," Al said. "See you in a few days, Mo, and we'll study the first chapter of I Peter. 5:30 am. Sharp."

That's what Al read this morning, Bob realized.

10

One life is all we have and we live it as we believe in living it.
But to sacrifice what you are and to live without belief,
that is a fate more terrible than dying.
Joan of Arc

Later that day and back at Al's house, all Bob could talk about was Mo and his story. Richard was all ears. After dinner they cleaned the kitchen and moved to the living room to relax.

"So, Bob," Al asked, "what were the top three things that stood out to you from our conversation with Mo today?" Al had a way of making Bob think, and it usually made him uncomfortable.

Bob gave it a thought and said, "First, his story is brutal! I can't imagine what he went through and I can't believe he can talk about it. I was also impressed with his honesty. He's so real. But the one I can't get over is how he said he was able to forgive the guy who killed his wife. I don't think that's possible. I sure couldn't do it."

"You might be right, Bob." Al said. "Sometimes it's not possible for us to forgive. It wasn't possible for Mo until he gave his life to Jesus. Even then, forgiveness didn't happen instantly. It's a process and he's come a long way. Could you see how his outlook on life changed when he put his faith in Christ?"

"Here we go with the Jesus thing again," thought Bob.

"Yeah, and that's great for him," Bob said. "But I'm not there yet."

"No pressure on you, my friend," Al said, kindly. "I'm only asking because I know you're hurting. You've hit a wall and I believe Jesus can get you through that wall. But I can't force you to believe him. Did you notice that you talked about someone other than yourself today?" Al couldn't help asking. What do you think about that, Bob? Maybe you have a heart, after all!"

Al's gentle teasing didn't bother Bob like it might have in the past. In fact, he realized thinking of someone else had actually lifted the dark cloud he was living under. However, when his thoughts returned to Lois and his own problems, the cloud settled on him again.

* * *

"Have you always lived in Sandusky, Bob?" asked Richard.

"Nope. Moved here from West Virginia. Coal country. My wife and I moved here shortly after we got married, so this is home now," Bob answered. "How about you guys? Now that you have the time, have you traveled much?"

"Never been east," Richard responded. "Al's been as far east as Pittsburg. I've been west as far as Wisconsin. We'd like to go farther west, but we need to save a few more pennies for that."

"How about you Bob? Have you and Lois traveled much?"

"Not really. Occasionally we get back to West Virginia. I've been to Canada fishing with my son..." Bob's voice trailed off.

The room quieted for a moment.

Bob continued. "That's about all the traveling we've done. Between work and injuries, we've stayed close to home." As Bob spoke, he realized he had never asked his wife if she would enjoy traveling. Once again his selfish side was showing up.

Then Bob asked, "Tell me about Wisconsin. What's that like? I've heard it's an amateur fisherman's version of Canada."

Richard laughed. "Good way to describe it. I haven't traveled the entire state but I drove through Milwaukee and along the Lake Michigan shore through Sheboygan, Green Bay and into Door County. It was a pretty long drive for me but I loved it. Door County was a nice combination of small villages and countryside with a lot of shoreline. I'm not a fisherman but I heard the fishing there is great.

That got Bob's attention. "What kind of fishing?"

"Well, in one of the restaurants both perch and walleye were on the menu. But I overheard some guys talking and I think they mentioned fishing for Salmon, Bass, and Muskie.

"Those are totally different types of fishing," Bob said. "Are you saying there's more than one fishing area?"

"I think so," he answered. "Door County is a peninsula so there would be fishing on the Lake Michigan side and also on the Green Bay side.

"That sounds great!" Bob's wheels were turning.

"If you're interested," Richard offered, "I've got pictures from that trip. I might even have a brochure of Door County."

"I'd love to see the pictures," Bob replied, eagerly.

Richard left the room and returned with a photo album. "The black and white pictures really don't do justice to the scenery. But the brochure has some nice colored pictures."

"Thanks. Do you mind if I look through these tonight?" Bob asked.

With that Al yawned and said, "You guys okay if I excuse myself? Think I'll go to bed."

Richard decided to follow his lead.

"Go ahead. See you in the morning," Bob said, holding the album.

Al smiled. "See you in the morning."

*   *   *

As soon as the brothers had gone to bed, Bob opened the album. Richard had been right about the quality of the photos, but they did capture some of the stunning shorelines. The brochure with the history of the county caught his attention.

The County of Door, Wisconsin, is a beautiful peninsula jutting out in a northeasterly direction into Lake Michigan, Bob read. It is eighteen miles wide at its base, gradually tapering to a width of approximately three miles at its northern boundary. It has 298 miles of shoreline varying from rocky bluffs to sandy beaches. It was home to several Native American tribal groups. Beginning in the 1800's, European settlers of Scandinavian, Belgian and German descent began arriving.

Bob could imagine spending time in Door County, fishing and relaxing. But in light of his current circumstances, he realized that was a pleasant though distant dream.

From the commercial fishing industry to sport fishing, the Friday night fish fry or fish boil, fishing has always been a huge part of the life of Door County.

The more Bob read, the more interested he became. He read about places with compelling names like Horseshoe Bay, Egg Harbor, Fish Creek, Ephraim, Sister Bay, Rowley's Bay, North Bay, Bailey's Harbor, JacksonPort, Whitefish Bay, Sturgeon Bay and Ellison Bay.

Then there was Riley's Bay and Sand Bay. Everywhere in the county were opportunities for recreation and rejuvenation. But what caught Bob's attention the most was something he read about Ellison Bay.

In the late 1940s, Bob read, a couple named Lawrence and Annette Wickman purchased a restaurant called the Viking Grill. They decided to try earning a living in the restaurant business by starting small and learning as they went. This appealed to Bob because he could understand the hard work it took to get it going and Bob was all about hard work.

In the summer 1961 the Viking served their first Fish Boil. Fish boils had their roots in a traditional Potawatomi feast. Filets of Whitefish were boiled in a large cast iron kettle over an open wood fire. The Viking added potatoes and onions to the pot and when the fish was ready, fuel would be added to the fire, causing a large flame to shoot toward the sky.

People loved the spectacle, and when the meal was served, everything was bathed in melted butter. Every year, the lines grew longer until as many as 700 people were served in an evening. Rye bread, coleslaw and cherry pie were added to complete the meal that was served outdoors, picnic style. Bob wondered what it would be like to meet the Wickmans who were still serving crowds at the Viking.

The next thing he knew Bob woke up in the same chair. It was two a.m. and he needed to clean up and get to bed.

* * *

Morning came too quickly for Bob, although he slept until almost eight. Richard and Al were enjoying their coffee when he walked into the kitchen. At Al's questioning look, he said, "I guess I got caught up reading about Door County and fell asleep in the chair. How far did you drive up the peninsula?" he asked Richard.

"I stayed in Fish Creek," Richard remembered, "but I drove all the way up to the tip of the peninsula. Not much up there, but trees and water. A few deer, I guess. It's pretty countryside."

"Did you eat at the Viking Grill?" Bob asked.

"Sure did!" he answered. "I was there Friday night for a Fish Boil. Outstanding!" he acclaimed.

Bob was hooked. He wasn't interested in cities or tourist towns.

The wide outdoors and plentiful fishing appealed to him. He was always looking to get away from folks.

Al interrupted his thoughts. "The clinic called today. They are going to release your wife this afternoon at three."

Bob's mind was jolted back from fantasizing about fish to facing facts. He tucked away the idea of Door County somewhere in the back of his mind.

"So Lois will be home tonight?"

"That's right Bob. After breakfast you can pack up and we can go over to your place and tidy it up before she gets home. Sound like a good plan?"

"Sure Al, whatever you think best." Bob hadn't thought about that.

11

Where we love is home – home that our feet may
leave, but not our hearts.
Oliver Wendall Homes, Sr

The two men arrived at Bob's home around ten. There wasn't much to do because Lois was a good housekeeper.

One of the first things Bob did was to open the refrigerator.

There were four cold Budweiser's and he handed them to Al.

"Probably not a good idea to have these around, right?" he mused.

"Probably not." Al agreed. He put the beer in a paper bag and they washed up the few dishes, mopped the kitchen floor and made sure everything was clean and organized in the other rooms.

Bob looked around, pleased with what he saw. "Lois loves a clean house, Al. She's going to like this."

"I hope so. But the bigger question is, will she like having you around?" Again, Al went right to the heart of the problem. "You've hurt her pretty bad and you need to handle this carefully."

A huge knot was forming in Bob's stomach. He knew Al was right. "Any suggestions?" he asked.

"Well, first we need to pray. Are you ok with that?" Bob was uncomfortable but said, "Sure."

Al bowed his head and prayed, *"Dear Father in heaven. You know all things and you are over all things. We need your help again today as we consider how best to approach Lois. She is hurting and we're at your mercy to understand our next steps. We want to do this in a way that honors you. In Jesus name we pray. Amen."*

Once again, Al's easy way of talking to God, as if he were right there in the room, was foreign to Bob. Most of the prayers Bob had heard were formal and read from a book.

"Let's go get some lunch and then pick up your wife."

"Are we eating out again?" Bob asked. "I hardly ever eat out."

"Why? Are you offering to cook?" Al smiled.

"Not a chance," Bob answered, realizing his question was ridiculous. He had no idea how to navigate his way around a kitchen.

Both men laughed and Al led the way to a diner for a quick lunch. At first Bob was suspicious of it being another set up, but Al didn't seem to know anyone in the diner.

*   *   *

It was only one thirty when they finished lunch and started toward the clinic.

"Aren't we going to get there a little early?" Bob asked.

"Nope." Al answered. "There will be some paperwork to fill out before she is released, but first we're going to stop at a florist. You need to let George Washington breathe and buy your wife some flowers!"

"Flowers?" Bob thought. He couldn't remember buying much for birthdays or holidays, let alone for no occasion. Besides, there were flowers left from Joey's funeral.

"I know, Bob." Al stated. "You think she's got plenty of flowers.

But this is different. They will be from you and they will be special. Don't expect her to acknowledge them, but I'm confident she will appreciate the gesture."

"If you say so," Bob said, doubtfully, "but I don't know anything about flowers. What kind should we get?"

"Roses."

The roses Al chose were the most expensive flowers in the shop. Bob winced when he saw the price. *"It's not his money,"* he thought, reluctantly. Put off by the cost, he dug into his wallet and finally paid the full amount.

Al strode up the sidewalk to the front door of the clinic while Bob lagged about three steps behind. He didn't know what to expect and he was tense.

"Come on, Bob. You'll be fine."

"I don't know," Bob said. "I'm pretty nervous."

"Good!"

The waiting room looked pretty *clinical* to say the least. The walls were lined with blue vinyl chairs with wooden arms, magazines were displayed on end tables and a receptionist sat behind the counter. Al greeted her and she handed him a folder. He walked them over to Bob and began to help him fill out the insurance and release forms. Bob had very little tolerance for paperwork but he managed to work his way through each one. When he finished, Al took the papers to the receptionist.

When Al returned he told Bob, "There, that's over. But from now on, you're on your own. I'm not gonna wipe your butt. Know want I mean?" Bob knew exactly what he meant.

A few minutes later the receptionist said everything was in order and they would be releasing Mrs. Chadwick soon. Nervously, Bob thumbed through some of the magazines on the table. Suddenly an article caught his attention. The title was *Door County, Wisconsin, The Hidden Jewel.*

He picked up the magazine and turned to the story.

On the first page was a large picture of a fisherman proudly holding up a good-sized small mouth bass. Just as Bob turned the page, the receptionist called out, "Mr. Chadwick, your wife is ready to be dismissed. She is in room 4."

Bob's stomach tightened up once again. "Al, are you coming with me?"

Al nodded. The two men walked down the hall floor to room 4 and Bob paused. Al looked at Bob.

"You first," Al said. "I'll be right behind you."

Bob took a deep breath and opened the door. "Hi, Lois." Lois turned her head away.

"Al and I are here to take you home." He held out the bouquet of a dozen red roses. When Lois saw Al she knew she would have to be civil to Bob, at least for now.

"My medicine is over there on the table. Can you reach it? And thanks for the flowers."

"Sure," Bob said awkwardly.

The three of them walked silently to the car and it was a quiet ride home. A few times Bob attempted to start a conversation, but he got one-word answers, so he gave up. When they arrived, he opened the door and helped Lois inside.

"Well, this is different!" Lois thought. When she walked into the kitchen she noticed the floor was shiny and the dishes were done and put away. "Did you do all this, Al?" she asked.

"Bob and I cleaned up together. Welcome home."

JERRY PRICE & TOM ROY

Lois walked into the living area and then the bedroom, surveying the tidy house. As she went to unpack her bag, she said, "You can leave my pills on the table, Bob."

"OK, will do."

Bob turned to Al. "What do I do now?" Al said, "How about you wait and see?"

Bob had never seen Lois like this and he had no idea how to act.

She was in control right now.

After what seemed like an hour, Lois came out of the bedroom. "You guys want some coffee?"

"That would be great," Al answered.

*   *   *

Lois found a package of cookies in the cupboard and within a few minutes they were sitting around the table with their coffee.

Finally, Lois broke the tension.

"So, I'm sure you both think I'm a nut cake."

"True," Bob thought, but didn't say anything.

Al was the one who answered. "Lois, you've had a rough go of it lately. And it doesn't help that you're married to this insensitive jerk." Lois was shocked, and so was Bob. Al gave him a look that said, *Be quiet!*

"If you were a guy, I'd probably call him a worse name. He hasn't treated you very well, has he?"

Lois didn't know Al very well. She'd only been around him in church and he'd seemed like nice enough man. Now she was seeing him in a new light. He seemed to have a lot of understanding.

"You have no idea," she said, bitterly. For years Lois had cowered under Bob's anger and tried to please him. It was never enough. When Joey died, something died in Lois as well. She stopped caring and no longer felt like trying.

Bob decided to speak up. "Honey, I'm really sorry you found me drunk. I know you needed me and I should have been there for you.

But I cleaned all the beer out of the fridge and I promise you I won't get drunk again. I hope you'll forgive me."

Lois wasn't buying it. "What do you mean you hope I'll forgive you? You didn't even ask! Sounds like you're just trying to look good in front of Al."

Then she gave Al a sardonic look and said, "You've trained your pet monkey well."

"Got any peanuts in the pantry?" Al asked her with a smile.

Bob felt like he'd been slapped but Al loved her response. It showed spunk. Lois was finally being honest about how she felt. With that, Al pushed back his chair.

"Well, I'll leave you two to sort out your relationship," he said. "Call me if you need help." It was time to leave. Lois could take care of herself.

Bob was stunned. "You're leaving already?"

"Yep. Gotta go," Al said. "The toilet paper is in the bathroom."

Lois looked puzzled but Bob got it. They both walked Al to the door and thanked him for his help.

"I'll be in touch soon," Bob said.

Al looked back and smiled. "Later."

12

"The battle you are going through is not fueled by the words or actions of others; it is fueled by the mind that gives it importance."
Shannon L. Alder

After Al left, things got quiet. It wasn't unpleasant but it was awkward. Finally Lois broke the tension.

"Bob, sometime we need to talk. The clinic helped me think through some things. What you did hurt deeply and I'm not ready to talk about it yet. Maybe in a couple of days but not right now.

Bob was okay with that. For now, he could ignore the inevitable 'talk.' His stomach eased as he realized he would have at least a day or two of peace.

"For now, if you could help me stay on schedule with my medicine, it would help. I'm supposed to take one with breakfast and one with supper. They help keep me even."

"Sure," Bob said, relieved. That was something he could do.

Her mention of supper triggered his hunger but he caught himself before asking Lois *"What's for supper?"* He had a hunch the timing might not be the best.

Instead, he asked, "Should we put these flowers in something?" "There's a vase in the cupboard above the stove." She pointed.

"And by the way, thank you. I don't think you've bought me flowers since Joey was born."

Speaking Joey's name had the same effect on both of them. It brought the atmosphere in the room down. Would the pain of grief ever ease?

Bob reached for the vase, added water and put the flowers in the middle of the kitchen table. Lois liked that spot.

"Would you like me to go out and get something for supper?" Bob offered.

"You're offering to go out and get us supper?" she asked, incredulously.

"Al took me to a place that butchers its own meat," he told her. "Does a hamburger sound good?"

"That's fine," she said, still unbelieving.

Bob had never done anything like this before. He hated spending money if there was a cheaper way. Lois would have loved eating out occasionally but Bob considered restaurants overpriced. He didn't consider the fact that although eating at home was cheaper, it meant more work for his wife.

Lois was skeptical about this new Bob and wondered if this was just a temporary adjustment to get her off his back. She wasn't in the mood for a burger, but since Bob had offered to get supper, she let it go."

"It's on the other side of town so it will take a bit, but I'll be back as soon as I can." Bob dashed out the door, on a mission.

* * *

Bob thought things were going pretty well, so far. Maybe soon he would be able to relax in his easy chair and enjoy his own home.When he arrived at the restaurant, there was Mo, larger than life, behind the counter. The place was just a little dive but already there were at least six tables with customers.

"Hey Bobby, you back already?" Mo called out, grinning.

Bob smiled. "Yeah, figured since I didn't get sick on that last burger I'd give you another chance. Can I get a couple of burgers for carry out?"

"Who the hell told you we do *carry out*? Whaddya think; this is some kind of fancy city place?"

It hadn't occurred to Bob they might not do carry out.

Mo continued, "Do you have any idea how much I have to pay for a paper bag to put your stuff in? I gotta wrap it all up like Christmas!"

Bob caught the hint of a smile on Mo's face.

"Take a seat." Mo said. "I'll take care of you when I can."

Bob sat down on a stool at the counter and after a couple of minutes Mo walked over, draping his arm over Bob's shoulder.

"How's life, Bobby?"

"Well, since you asked, Al and I just brought my wife home from the clinic. She's been working with a counselor. She thinks I'm a real asshole."

"So you pissed her off pretty good, I'm guessin'?"

"You could say that," Bob answered. "I haven't always been the easiest guy to be around."

Recalling what Mo had recounted about his wife's brutal rape and murder made Bob feel like a heel, so he said, "I need to appreciate her more, Mo."

"Probably a good idea," Mo agreed. "Now, what you want for carry out?"

"I'll take a couple of half pound burgers and a large order of fries."

"You sure your wife wants a burger?" Mo asked, looking sideways at Bob. Women like salad and stuff. How about a chicken sandwich and a side salad?"

"Great! She'll like that."

While Mo put the order together, Bob took in the customers and the simple décor.

A few minutes later Mo returned. "I threw in a few veggies for you guys," he said, as he handed Bob the bag. "My daughter has a friend with a garden and she just brought these in today."

"Thanks! That's nice of you. How is she?" "She seems fine."

"Good!" Bob replied. "How much I owe you?"

When Bob saw the bill he wondered if Mo had undercharged him. "You sure this is right?" he asked, handing over a few bills.

"Get out of here!" Mo laughed. "Your food's gettin' cold!"

Bob headed toward the door and then stopped. "Mo, can I ask you a favor?"

"My wife and I aren't doing too well. We're in some deep trouble. I don't really know what I believe but I know you believe in Jesus. Would you mind saying a prayer for me tonight?"

"Sure," Mo said, a little stunned. "That's a first but I'll be glad to. Thanks for asking."

"If God would listen to anyone, I think he'd listen to you. You seem to have a real honest relationship with him."

"No problem." Mo was honored. "Now get outta here before that food gets cold!"

Bob left, feeling better for being honest with Mo.

*   *   *

When Bob walked through the door he found the table set and Lois waiting for him. He had to admit that the flowers seemed to cheer up the place. Although it was simple food, they both felt a sense of hope that evening.

JERRY PRICE & TOM ROY

"I got you a chicken sandwich and a side salad," Bob said, placing the food on the table. I hope it's okay. I remembered you're not a huge fan of burgers."

Lois was pleasantly surprised. Could this be a good sign?

"Thank you, Bob. This is exactly what I would have chosen." They ate in silence, but it wasn't bad. They were together.

When they were finished, Bob threw away the wrappers and started filling the sink with hot water and soap.

Lois watched as Bob put the plates and silverware in the sink. "You've never done that before, Bob," she said quietly.

"Can't say never," Bob said good-naturedly. "I washed the dishes at Al's house. Like you said, I'm his trained monkey."

As she went to her favorite chair in the living room, Lois was thankful but she wondered how long this new Bob would last.

"Where did you get this book on Door County?"

"Al's brother loaned it to me. Looks like a neat place."

As Bob finished up in the kitchen, Lois browsed through the book. She thought, *Bob's acting totally different, at least for tonight.*

13

"Crying is all right in its way while it lasts. But you have to stop sooner or later, and then you still have to decide what to do."
C.S. Lewis, The Silver Chair

It was three days before Lois felt ready to talk. Bob was outside working on the lawn mower and fantasizing about fishing in Door County. When he walked into the house he could see by the look on his wife's face that she was ready to talk. Mentally, he put on his miner's helmet.

"I am guessing it's time to talk?" he asked.

"You know this isn't going to be easy," she said. "I want to be honest and I'm asking you to just listen for now."

Bob sensed this was going to be painful. He knew he had done some hurtful things but it wasn't *all* his fault, was it?

"For a long time I feel we've just *existed* together," she began. "I've been quiet most of the time so you wouldn't blow up. But you get angry even when I don't speak up."

Lois paused and began again. "It's been this way for a long time, but when Joey died, something changed. I really don't care anymore if you get mad or not."

She began reminding him of some of his many offenses, like his lack of help when Joey was born, the way he treated her when Joey started school, the punch to Charley's face at the mill.

There was also the way he was so tight with money, the magazines in the shed, his drinking, and the list continued.

"*This could be a long night,*" Bob groaned inwardly. The one incident they had never talked about was the most hurtful of all, but Dr. Kennedy had strongly encouraged her to tell Bob how she felt.

"Bob, do you remember the time you were working outside and you yelled at me to come out and help you move the picnic table?" she asked.

He winced.

"You stepped on one of your tools that *you* left on the ground," she accused. "You tripped and the table fell on my ankle. I was hurt and you were mad you had to stop what you were doing and drive me to the ER."

"Bob," she continued, quietly, "my ankle was hurt but it was nothing compared with the pain of learning I had miscarried."

Lois couldn't speak for a moment. "All you could think about," she choked out, "was how much the hospital visit was going to cost."

Bob felt like a caged animal, desperate to escape. He sure wished he had a couple of *buds* in the fridge right now!

"Learning we had lost our daughter was when I began to lose hope," she said. "There isn't a day I don't think about our little girl. I wonder what she would have looked like. I think about what it would have been like to read to her, fix her hair, bake together and even plan her wedding. I was robbed of all that, Bob."

Lois began to cry.

Bob saw the pain in his wife. He hadn't thought much about that day. He was beginning to realize how deeply Lois felt about family.

"Then you went off to Canada with our only son and came back without him. You've ruined my life, Bob!" Lois said, bitterly.

After that comment, Bob lost his cool. "You're blaming me for Joey's death?" he shouted. "Do you really think I had anything to do with it? Don't you think I'm hurting just as much as you?"

Lois looked up at Bob and shouted back. "Whatever happened, I no longer have a son or a daughter!" Clearly, she matched Bob's anger.

Suddenly the room grew silent, and somehow the silence seemed louder than their shouting.

*   *   *

Lois was right. They were a married couple that never truly knew each other. They had just *existed*. Though they lived in a comfortable house with a comfortable lifestyle, neither had any idea how to have an authentic relationship. Now they were in a crisis and they were just beginning to realize the significance of what had happened. Another wave of pain came over Lois.

"And then you came home and drowned yourself in beer!" Lois added. "It was pretty clear the only person you were thinking about was yourself!"

"I may not show it much, Lois, but I do have a heart!" Bob remembered how he had worried about what to say to Lois. He had felt helpless, which was his excuse to reach for his *buds*.

Then out of the blue, he asked, "And who the hell was that guy who winked at you at the viewing?"

Lois looked up. "What are you talking about?"

"You know exactly what I am talking about. One of the guys from Coaltown gave you a *look!*" Bob knew he was changing the direction of the conversation, but it felt good to take back control.

"He's just an old friend from high school," she said, looking down.

Bob kept questioning her and she knew she was losing ground. Finally, she broke down.

"The night before we got engaged, I went out with him. He had a bottle of wine in his truck. I had a little too much to drink and he took advantage of me. It was a one night fling."

Bob went ballistic! "Took advantage of you? What does that mean?"

"He started kissing me and putting his hands all over me," she finally answered, but that's all."

"That's all?" Bob yelled. "And you didn't think you should tell me this before now?"

Lois was a mess. She was crying hard and curled up in a ball. "Well," he said angrily, "you sure know how to throw fuel on a fire!" Bob had been holding himself in check for several days and something about his anger felt *good* to him. He had turned the focus on *her* faults.

Lois was sobbing uncontrollably.

"I'm sorry, Bob," she started to say. "I guess I should have told you..." but Bob was walking out of the room in a rage.

Bob's anger on top of the reality she would never see her children again convulsed her in pain. Bob saw her double over as he slammed the screen door. *"A beer sure would taste good right now,"* he thought. *"Maybe a dozen!"*

Bob was reverting back to his old ways of dealing with life and he knew it. *I have a right to be angry*, he thought. *"She betrayed me!"*

He'd been wronged and he wanted to nurse his hurt. Oddly, he found himself sitting at the same table he had dropped on Lois the day she lost the baby. Without his beer, the memory of that day slowly came into focus and he began to loath himself. He was starting to see how Lois saw him and he hated it.

Their talk had been brutally honest, exposing a lot of ugliness, but there was something in Bob that yearned for a marriage with that kind of honesty, with no secrets. In his heart, however, he knew it would have to begin with him.

* * *

Eventually, Bob walked back into the house. Lois was still crying softly and he waited.

"What?" she asked, looking up at him.

"I know I've been a jerk and I'm sorry. I don't know where all this talking will go but I want to stay together and I want to keep talking. Is that what you want, too?"

Lois was surprised but she heard Bob's heart. He hadn't told her what to do; he had given her a choice!

* * *

They continued talking late into the night, sometimes sharing hurts, sometimes weeping together. Neither of them had thought life would turn out this way. What did the future look like? Was there even a future for them?

It was well past midnight and Lois was exhausted. They had talked through some difficult things, but there was something else on her mind. And she knew she needed to bring it up because she might not have the courage later.

It was risky, knowing Bob might not react well, but she didn't want to feel responsible for his temper any more. She didn't want to mop up his messes. Even though she hadn't heard

Al's remark, she didn't want to *diaper his hind end* any more, either!

"Bob," she began cautiously, "I've been thinking we should become foster parents. I'd like to ask for a girl."

Bob, who was beginning to feel worn down, was wide-awake now!

"Are you kidding me?" he thought. *"Where the hell did that come from?"*

It was an abrupt change in course and his thoughts were tumbling together. *So much for my privacy! And there goes my savings account! A foster child? A girl?*

"I won't even be able to walk out of the bedroom in my underwear!" Bob blurted out.

Lois looked puzzled. *"Where did that come from?"* she thought. She did her best not to react to such a strange comment because she could tell he was frightened.

Bob's mind kept manufacturing all the reasons to resist until another thought hit him. Lois' desire to have a foster child revealed she wanted to stay together and make a go of their marriage.

* * *

The thought of taking in someone else's kid wasn't appealing to Bob, especially one with baggage. As he was contemplating this, Lois dropped another surprise on him.

"Since we're getting older, I'd like her to be about the same age our daughter would have been. I'd like to find a girl between fourteen and seventeen.

"Oh boy," thought Bob. *"Here we go! Teenage hormones! This is crazy!"*

Bob didn't express how he felt. Instead, he said, "It's late. Let's go to bed and talk about this when we've had some rest."

Although they shared a bed, they didn't touch each other.

* * *

The next day they were polite but cool toward each other.

Finally at supper Lois brought up the dreaded subject.

"Have you thought any more about a foster daughter, Bob?" This was a different Lois than Bob had known, much bolder than before.

"A little," he replied, "but I don't feel like talking about it now." The emotional chill remained in the home.

A few days later Lois' mood seemed a little lighter. "I'm going into town to do some shopping." She was looking at the weekly ad for the grocery store in the morning paper. "We need groceries and they have a good price on roast beef."

Bob offered, "How about if I drive you into town? I can do a few errands while you're at the store."

Lois thought for a moment and decided it was a good plan.

As Bob pulled into a parking space in front of the grocery store, he said, "I'm going to take a walk. I should be back in about thirty minutes."

"Ok, see you here in about thirty minutes," she said.

Bob walked the block and a half to the local hardware store and spent the entire time wandering the aisles. He picked up a screwdriver and a few batteries for his flashlight.

He and Lois met each other at the car. "Good timing," she said.

As he loaded the car with groceries, Lois handed him a

paper. "This is a brochure on foster care. I thought you might like to look it over."

"Man," he thought, *"She's not giving up on this!"* He was still nursing his wound about Lois giving herself to the guy from Coaltown and he was not willing to give in.

* * *

That evening Lois asked him if he had looked at the brochure.

He hadn't.

"If we ever decide to look into this, and I'm not saying we are, how long would we have to keep her?" Bob asked as he picked up the brochure. "Can we give her back if we don't like her?"

Lois was shocked that he sounded as if he might actually consider it, so she ignored the insensitivity in his question.

"I don't know the answer to that, but I'm sure we can find out," she responded.

* * *

Later that same week, Bob and Lois found themselves at the office of Child Protective Services. They were greeted by a Mrs. Smithson who was kind, helpful, and answering all their questions. As she guided them through the application, she gave them some background on the foster system.

"If you are approved to become foster parents, you need to know the state will help you with child related expenses."

Now *that* was something Bob was happy to hear! As they left, Lois seemed to be happier than he'd seen her in years.

Bob wasn't sold on the idea yet, but they had taken the first step and it had put a bounce in his wife's step. He couldn't believe he was even considering this. Would they really go through with it?

* * *

Six weeks later, Lois got her wish for a girl. Lois would never forget that September day when they went to pick up Sandra. They had repainted Joey's room, which hadn't been touched since his death. It was one thing Bob had insisted on if they were going to go through with this.

It was all happening too fast for Bob. But he had a plan. He saw how Lois had a glow on her face and knew she would be a wonderful foster mother, making sure the girl had everything she needed. All he had to do was put up with *that girl* for now.

Bob's plan involved gradually teaching the girl to take over most of his chores. She was old enough to cut the lawn, weed the garden, pick the vegetables as well as helping with household jobs. He would have more time in his easy chair!

Lois quickly doused that dream. "I read many foster children feel like the only reason they were brought into the home was to be a servant," she said. "We need to be careful not to make Sandra feel that way. In fact, I want her to feel like a princess!"

Bob's plans were eroding, but he held out hope. Maybe by winter when it was time to shovel snow, Lois would forget about her princess plan.

Sandra was about five foot six and looked about twenty pounds overweight to Bob. She didn't wear anything fancy but was by no means sloppy. She had red hair with a smattering of freckles and Lois was absolutely in love with her! Bob could see he was *not* going to be the center of his wife's attention and he wondered how much this girl was going to change his life.

14

"I think most of us are raised with preconceived notions of the choices we're
supposed to make...Nobody says, 'Just be happy –
go be a cobbler or go live with goats."
Sandra Bullock

The house felt and looked different. It even *smelled* different. Bob and Sandra got along fine, at least for the first few weeks. He noticed Sandra loved being treated like a princess. She was blossoming and Lois was happy but Bob felt like in a household of three, he ranked about tenth. Yes, Bob was jealous. His resentment had been building and he was getting close to his boiling point.

One day when he and Sandra were both in the kitchen, he spilled some coffee grounds and he asked Sandra to get the broom.

"Do it yourself, Bob," she retorted. "I'm not your maid."

Bob boiled over. "Just who do you think you are?" he demanded, glaring at her.

"The one keeping your marriage together, she answered," without hesitation.

Bob was speechless!

"Lois and I are very close," she continued. "She told me about Joey and about losing the baby. I know all about it. So get your own broom, *Bob!*"

He was livid. Why would Lois talk about such personal things to this girl he barely knew. Later that evening he confronted his wife.

"What were you thinking, Lois," Bob demanded, "telling Cinderella all about our life? She's not family!"

"We can talk about anything we want," she shot back. Lois wasn't backing down. "It's nice to have someone around here that cares!"

Bob's life began to take a subtle turn. As the relationship between Lois and Sandra grew closer, his marriage was growing further apart.

* * *

From the time Sandra became a part of the scenery, Bob met with Al to discuss his home life. He would relate how Lois and Sandra seemed to have a fairly normal mother daughter relationship.

For Bob, however, Sandra was a foster child and would never be a real daughter. She was seventeen when she came to live with them and soon she would be out of the system and on her own. He wanted Lois to be happy but in his gut something didn't seem quite right about Sandra.

At first, he shrugged it off as just his jealousy over how close she was with Lois. He couldn't forget the way Sandra had served him notice in the kitchen about who was in charge. And he didn't like the way she and Lois had teamed up against him. In his mind, he thought his wife had betrayed him once again. Sadly, as Bob and Lois grew more distant, they began to keep secrets from each other, which took a toll on their marriage.

When Bob talked about Lois and Sandra, Al would always try to point the discussion toward Jesus, but Bob wasn't ready to listen. He knew he was being selfish but he felt justified.

Every night Bob would lie awake trying to figure out how to fix things. He was losing confidence in Al's ability to really see what was going on. He didn't tell Al, but as far as he was concerned, he just wanted to get out of the situation. Finally, he began to devise a plan.

After a week of careful thought, it was time to put his plan into action. It was a beautiful October day and Lois was taking Sandra into town to shop for fall clothes. Normally Bob would have grumbled about spending money, but this time he gave them plenty to buy what they wanted. While the girls were shopping, Bob took the old car they had purchased for Sandra and made a quick stop at the bank, withdrawing all but $500 from his savings account. He had a secret plan and it was time to pull it off.

Next stop, Door County!

*   *   *

No more competing with Lois for her time. No more footing the bill for a girl he barely knew. Lois would be fine. She had her new best friend. He had left her a little money and she could continue to collect his unemployment check. In his mind, she would be fine.

He was done. He felt a little guilty about leaving Al, who had been there for him, but frankly he was tired of all the Jesus talk. Most important to Bob, he was now free to start over! He was confident he could find a job that would earn him enough to live on.

He wrote Lois a note and left it on the table.

"So long, Lois. Have fun with Cinderella. I'm out of here. I've caused you plenty of pain and now you've paid me back. Maybe I'll be in touch when I land somewhere." Bob

* * *

The old Ford had lots of miles on it and leaked oil. Bob had to stop every so often to check the oil level. He hoped the car could make the trip. But even that couldn't put a damper on his excitement. He had done it! He had pulled off his great escape and he felt free for the first time in as long as he could remember. It was the fall of 1974 and he was about to begin an exciting, new life.

Bob had carefully studied the book about Door County and was especially interested in Ellison Bay. Although it was near the tip of the peninsula and was farther away, it was exactly what Bob was looking for to start his life over. He felt light as he thought about all the good times ahead. When he crossed the Illinois border, Bob shouted out his window, "Hello Door County, here I come!"

Traveling through Chicago slowed things down a bit and Bob was feeling road weary. *"Man, my butt is getting sore! I hope the roads are better in Wisconsin."*

He was not so lucky. The long Wisconsin winters left the roads rough with potholes. He was in for more hard miles and the trip took longer than he anticipated.

* * *

Finally, Bob pulled into the parking lot of a small 'mom and pop' motel just north of Milwaukee, ready for a good meal and some much needed rest. As he walked into the office, it was clear this wasn't an upscale accommodation. A large woman with bleached hair and cigarette stains on her fingers commanded the motel office.

"Good evening, sir, what can I do for ya?"

"I need a room for the night. Any openings?" Bob asked.

"We do have a room available, but it's our honeymoon suite."

"Who would want to stay in a place like this on their honeymoon," Bob wondered. "Do you get many honeymooners here?" he asked aloud.

"Well, that's what they tell us," she answered with a wink. "How much?" he asked, cautiously.

When she told him the price, it seemed fair and he agreed. He took the key, picked up his duffle bag and made his way to the 'suite' at the far end of the motel. Once inside, he found a full size bed with a pink floral print on the bedding and drapes.

"You gotta be kidding me!" he thought, but it seemed clean enough so he unpacked his few belongings and made his way back to the office.

"Any suggestions on where to eat?" he asked the woman at the desk.

"You want fancy or filling?" she asked.

"I'll go with filling," he answered with a chuckle.

"Turn left out of the parking lot, go two miles to the service station and take a right. About a block down is Juicy Lucy's. They'll treat you right. Tell them Marge sent ya."

"Juicy Lucys?" Bob wondered if the food would be safe to eat!

It was nothing fancy on the outside but Lucy's looked OK. When he walked inside, the place was packed. The room was full of smoke and people turned their heads to watch as Bob made his way to the only available table.

"Something to drink?" the bartender looked up at him, listing the beer on tap.

"What else ya got?" Bob shot back.

"What else is there?" the bartender asked. "You're in Wisconsin!"

Bob ordered a Schlitz.

A middle-aged waitress slapped a menu down in front of him and he asked what she suggested. "It's all good," she answered, "but I'd go with a *brat*. Comes with raw or fried onions."

Bob wasn't sure what a brat was, so he said, "Just bring me a cheeseburger."

"Cheddar ok?" she asked. Before he could answer she turned and yelled, "Gimme a burger with cheddar." Turning back to Bob, she asked, "Fries or onion rings?"

"Uh, fries, I guess. By the way, Marge said to tell you she sent me."

The waitress looked at Bob indifferently and said, "Whaddya want, a medal?"

Waiting for his food, Bob watched the customers, happily drinking their beer. There were almost as many women as men, which kind of surprised him. This wasn't what he was used to in Sandusky, but he decided to embrace his new environment. *"Different is what I need,"* he thought to himself.

* * *

Minutes later the waitress returned with a cheeseburger as big as a child's head. "*That's* a big burger!" he observed.

"That's the kiddie size," she joked. "Gotta work your way up to real food." Then she asked him where he was from.

"Why?" Bob asked, wondering how she could tell he wasn't a local.

"Your accent." She replied.

Accent? Bob didn't think he had one. In fact, he thought the same thing about her. Then, looking down at his plate, he wondered if he could eat it all.

Reading his mind, she laughed, "Just order a few more beers to wash it down." He went through three more beers and finished all but a few fries.

"Wanna doggie bag for those?" the waitress asked, with a crooked smile.

"No thanks, just the bill."

He was a little wobbly when he stood, but he felt good. Bob was back to what felt normal for him. The Schlitz was a bit different from his Budweiser, but it still did the trick. His belly was full, his mind was numb and there was no one to make him feel guilty. He put his money on the counter and made his way back to his room.

*   *   *

Bob was out the minute he hit the bed, oblivious to the pink floral covers. Grabbing a quick cup of coffee in the motel office the next morning, he paid his bill and was on the road by six a.m., ready to take on his great adventure. In a few hours he would be in Door County, Wisconsin.

The trip took a bit longer than he had hoped. After navigating through traffic in Milwaukee, an accident near Grafton slowed traffic almost to a stop.

Finally he broke free of the congestion and continued north, past Sheboygan. At Manitowoc, he turned east toward the lakeshore, following highway 42 toward Door County, taking him through small towns like Two Rivers and Kewaunee.

Bob noticed the landscape was changing. Pristine farms dotted the countryside, and the woods were filled with birch, cedar and spruce. Occasionally the view opened up on his right, revealing glimpses of the sparkling blue of Lake Michigan. He followed the signs pointing toward Sturgeon Bay.

As he descended the hill toward the bridge crossing its bay, he noticed the enormous cargo ships, tugs and personal craft for sailing, fishing or pleasure.

This is my kind of place! Bob thought. Since it was close to lunchtime, he started looking for a place to eat. According to his map, Ellison Bay was still an hour away.

15

"When your values are clear to you, making decisions becomes easier."
Roy E. Disney

Turning left on Third Avenue, Bob spotted a blue sign that said, "The Nautical." It was definitely a step up from Lucy's. The lunch crowd had thinned out but there were a few customers sitting at the bar. Bob joined them, admiring the dark, polished wood.

"What can I get ya?" the man behind the bar asked. "Do you have Schlitz on tap?" he asked.

"Coming up!" The bartender slid the cold drink across the bar. "You from around here?" the bartender asked with a quizzical look.

"Nope." Bob said, wondering if his *accent* had tipped the man off. "Ohio, but hoping to settle around here."

"Family?" the man asked.

"Just me," Bob replied.

"Okay," the bartender shrugged, glancing at Bob's wedding ring. "Well, let me know if you need anything," he continued. "I've lived here my whole life. Know most folks around here so if you need any leads, let me know."

"Might just take you up on that!" Bob answered, gratefully. "Name's Bob. What's yours?"

"I'm Karl Schmidt," the man replied, extending his hand. "Welcome to my tavern."

When the bartender left to fill another man's drink, Bob pulled off his wedding ring and slid it into his pocket.

Karl seemed like a good guy, the type Bob would hang out with. When he returned, Bob asked, "Got anything worth eating in this tavern?"

"We pride ourselves on our brats. They come straight from Sheboygan, the bratwurst capital of the country! We top it with fried onions. If you want something fancier, try our grilled cheddar sandwich," he said.

"Does everyone up here serve brats?" Bob asked.

"Yeah, pretty much. Along with beer." Both men laughed. "You need a refill?"

"Sure, and I'll try a brat." "Fried onions?"

"Sure, why not? What else you recommend?" "Mustard and beer!" Karl smiled.

"I'd better take it easy on the beer," Bob said. "I've still got a little drive ahead."

Bob was sold on brats. The bun was lightly dusted in cornmeal and the bratwurst was seasoned well and grilled to perfection.

"This is really good!" he said, taking another bite.

"Ya know, after your fifth brat you're eligible for Wisconsin citizenship," Karl announced. Bob knew he was joking.

"Where ya headed?" Karl asked.

"Ellison Bay."

"That's only about an hour from here. If ya get pulled over, it'll be my Uncle Harold. He's the only cop on duty today. Just tell him Karl got you loaded and he'll wave you on."

Bob's eyes widened. *"I think I'm going to like this place!"* he thought. Restraint gave way after his second beer and before Bob knew it, he was pretty much in the bag.

"Any good looking women up here?" he asked.

"Sure, but most of them are either married or they've got a few miles on them," Karl answered, with a sideways grin.

"I like working on high mileage vehicles." Bob said. They both laughed.

Karl could see Bob was past the ability to operate a vehicle. We've got rooms upstairs," he offered.

"I'm f-f-fine. I can *dive*. I mean *drive*." Bob slurred.

"Don't think so, Bob." Karl helped him up the stairs, but not before Bob insisted on 'one more' to take along in case he got lonely. It was only four in the afternoon, but Bob was down for the count.

Around nine that evening, he woke up to use the bathroom, having no idea where he was. He bumped off the wall, relieving himself in the wastebasket, and fell back on the bed in a deep sleep. He was awakened at one a.m. to loud music downstairs and a bit more clarity. He was beginning to remember where he was.

"Man, this place smells like piss!" he thought. Slowly, he pulled on his pants, smoothed his hair and went downstairs. Karl was still behind the bar.

Looking up at Bob, he said, "Hey, how're ya feelin'?"

"Fine." Bob lied. "You got cows up there? Smells like a barn."

"Might be your breath!" thought Karl. He knew it was the beer talking, so he let it go. "Nope. Plenty of cows here in Door but we keep 'em outdoors."

A guy at the bar laughed.

"Got any more beer?" Bob asked.

"Sure," Karl replied. "But first, how about you tally up for last night?"

Bob let out a low belch. "No problem." He pulled out a large roll of bills. "This should cover it."

"Put your money away," Karl said, eyeing the wad of cash. "I'll keep a tab and you can pay up in the morning."

"Good, 'cuz I'm thirsty." Several beers later, Bob stumbled upstairs. The next thing he remembered was waking to the sun coming through the blinds and the smell of coffee.

*　*　*

"Coffee?" Karl asked, when Bob found his way to a table.

Bob nodded. His head was pounding and his eyes were blurry.

"You the only one that ever works here?" he asked, as Karl poured the steaming coffee.

"Pretty much." Karl looked away. "The wife couldn't take the hours. She took off with a guy from Crivitz. Never said goodbye."

Ouch! thought Bob. "Sorry to hear that."

"Hey, that's life." Karl shrugged. "So what's your story?" Bob liked this guy, but he wasn't about to open up to him.

"Well, I used to work in a steel mill and got injured, so I had to retire. My old lady is nuts and I needed some space."

"So your wife's in an institution?"

"In and out," he said, vaguely. "Hey, what do I owe you?" Bob was eager to change the subject.

"The room is on me. Twenty four bucks for the brat and the beer," Karl said. Then with a smile, he added, "not including the tip."

"Shit! How did I run up a tab like that?" Bob was shocked. He had no idea how much beer he had consumed.

"You didn't eat much, but you did buy a few rounds for everyone."

Bob nodded and paid his tab. "Sorry, didn't mean to cuss." "Don't worry about it," Karl waved his hand dismissively. "I've heard worse language from preachers around here!"

"Better get moving," Bob said, stretching his legs. "Any advice on where to stay?"

"Not much up there but fishermen," Karl answered. "You might ask around and see if anyone has a fishing shack you could rent."

"Thanks for everything." Bob headed for the door, eager to explore Ellison Bay. "See you again, I hope."

"You're welcome any time," Karl waved. "Make sure you tell people you're only four brats away from citizenship. Your beer card is already full."

16

"For last year's words belong to last year's language.
And next year's words await another voice.
And to make an end is to make a beginning."
(Little Gidding)
T.S. Eliot

As Bob followed highway 42 North out of Sturgeon Bay, he took in the acres of apple and cherry orchards. In the tiny town of Egg Harbor, he caught his first glimpse of Green Bay waters. He couldn't wait to drop a fishing line in *that* pond!

Winding through the charming villages, he was aware of the family resorts and the tourist shops, but what appealed to Bob were the cozy harbors and assortment of boats. This was a fisherman's paradise!

He decided to take a detour in Fish Creek, turning in at the entrance to Peninsula State Park. He figured he had a little time to see the sights. The view of Weborg Point was stunning, with Gibraltar Bluff rising up behind the village. He drove past wooded campsites and the Eagle Bluff lighthouse. This was a different world from Sandusky. Everything seemed so primeval and he loved it.

Descending into Ephraim, he saw the twin steeples of the Moravian Church and the old schoolhouse, standing like sentinels overlooking Eagle Harbor. Later he learned that the sale of alcohol was prohibited in Ephraim, making it the only dry town in the entire state. "

Guess I won't be spending much time here!" Bob mused. In his mind, the only reason for coming to Ephraim was to stop at Wilson's for ice cream. He headed north toward Sister Bay.

Next to Sturgeon Bay, Sister Bay was the county's largest town on the peninsula. It had a hotel, a bowling alley and a few restaurants. The road wound along the bay through an attractive residential area.

* * *

Finally, Bob rolled into Ellison Bay. He knew the first thing on his agenda was finding a place to stay, but his stomach reminded him he hadn't eaten breakfast. The only restaurant he saw in town, which was only a few blocks along highway 42, was The Viking.

Bob recalled what he had read about this restaurant in the book he had borrowed from Al's brother, Richard. It was to become his breakfast spot for many a morning to come.

There was nothing fancy about The Viking, but it was clean and he was greeted warmly.

"What can I get ya to drink, der?" the waitress asked placing a menu in front of him.

"I'd like a glass of milk," he answered, looking around at the other tables. There was an older couple at one table and a group of men at another, sipping coffee and having an animated conversation.

One of the men, wearing overalls and an untrimmed beard, got up and approached Bob's table, singing.

"*I know you deceived me now here's a surprise.*" He had a deep, raspy voice and a vacant look. "Name the song and the artist!"

Without waiting for an answer, the man went back to his table and sat down.

The waitress returned with a large glass of milk. "What can I get you?"

"I'll take the brat patty and 2 eggs, over easy. Wheat toast," he answered. It was late enough to have ordered lunch, but he was curious about the brat patty.

As she scribbled his order on a pad, he asked in a hushed voice, "Who's that man over there with the beard?"

"Oh, that's Timothy Czech. He's in here all the time. He was in a car accident several years ago and he's never been the same. I'm sure he asked you to name a song."

"He did," Bob answered, surprised. "What's that all about?" "It's just his thing. Any time someone comes in here alone, he sings a line from a song. He gives them until they finish their food to come up with the song title and the artist. Just play along; he's harmless."

"Okay," Bob said. "That's a first for me."

"Quite a few of the folks up here are *unique*," she said, with a sideways smile. "I'm guessing you'll fit right in."

"I like her," Bob thought.

When his food arrived she asked if he needed anything else. "Yes," he answered. "What's your name?"

"Wanda," she answered. "Why? Are you hitting on me?" she asked, laughing and adding that she was happily married, most of the time.

"Glad to hear," was all Bob could think of to say.

"If you come in here much, you'll figure out which days I *don't* feel so happily married," she offered.

When Bob finished his meal he was still a bit hungry. Catching Wanda's eye, he asked, "What do you have for dessert?"

"If you like cherry pie, you're at the right place. The apple pie isn't bad, either."

"I'll take a piece of that cherry pie."

Wanda was right! That pie was the best cherry pie he'd ever had. When he finished, she met him at the cash register.

"Guess I'll be seeing you again," he said. "I like this place."

"Try the Whitefish chowder," she suggested.

As he opened the door to leave, Bob paused and called back inside the restaurant. "*I Can See for Miles and Miles,* by The Who."

Timothy smiled.

* * *

As Bob drove slowly through the town, he searched for a place to stay. He was looking for a spot to bed down, hopefully for the rest of his life.

Spotting a building with Klenke's Garage painted on the front, he decided to stop in. He remembered his dad telling him when he was a kid that every man needed a mechanic for a friend.

He parked his car in front of the door and stepped out. When he walked inside he didn't see anyone so he poked his head around the corner.

"Anyone here?"

"Yeah, hold on. I'll be right with you," said a voice from underneath an old pickup truck. Gus Klenke slid out from under the truck, wiped his hands on an old rag and looked at Bob.

"Gus," he said, extending his hand. "How can I help ya?"

"Name's Bob. And I'm looking for a place to stay. I had a hunch you might be able to help. Besides, it never hurts to have a mechanic for a friend. You never know when you might need a good deal on car repairs."

Bob was joking and fortunately the guy got it.

Gus had inherited the garage from his dad. He was a hardworking man and the locals respected him.

"So ya need a friend, do ya?" "S'pose I do," Bob responded. "You from *Illinois?*"

"Nope." Bob said. "Sandusky, Ohio." It was an odd question. "Glad to meet ya, then." Bob wondered if there was bad blood between Wisconsin and Illinois.

"What model Ford do you drive," Gus asked. "How do you know I drive a Ford?

"Because you said you might need a mechanic," he answered. "I see a lot of Fords in here."

They both laughed.

"Yeah, I do drive a Ford," Bob laughed. "It's the old one out front."

Gus looked out the window and nodded, "I'm sure that car and I will become good friends. Now, what can I do for you?"

"I need a place to stay. I've just had a good meal at The Viking and now I'm looking for a good bed."

"The Viking, eh?" Gus said. "How's Wanda today?" "She seemed fine to me."

She's a fine woman. Did you meet Timothy?" "Sure did.

"Do you know everyone in town?"

"Pretty much," said Gus. "So you need a place to live. How picky are ya?" Gus asked.

"For a few nights I could sleep pretty much anywhere. But eventually, I'll need something more permanent."

"So you're planning to stay here awhile?"

"Yep, I hope to settle down here."

Gus was curious why a single guy in his mid-forties would choose to live in Ellison Bay. It was a place where kids grew up and left for bigger things.

"You know about the winters here?"

"We have winter in Ohio, too," Bob said.

"He has no idea what real winter looks like," Gus thought. "Well, we can save the small talk. You need a place to sleep."

Bob could see the wheels turning in Gus' head. "Got any money?"

"I can get by for a little while, but I was hoping to pick up a few odd jobs once I get settled."

"You'll fit right in," Gus told him. Most folks in Door work several jobs. You know anything about fishing?"

"I love fishing." Bob hoped he didn't sound too eager. "Great." Bob wondered what Gus had in mind. "Now let's see what we can do about a place for a few days."

With that Gus picked up the phone. It was a party line, so he waited until the other party finished and dialed a number. After a brief conversation he handed Bob an address.

"These people will set you up for the next few days," Gus looked Bob in the eye. "Meet me for breakfast in the morning and we'll figure out the rest." He wanted to know who this guy was and why he wanted to move to Ellison Bay.

"Where do you want to meet?" Bob asked.

Gus chuckled. "Well, let's see. How about six at the Viking? Or we could meet in Milwaukee if you prefer."

Bob thanked Gus for the help. "See you at six sharp."

The address Gus gave Bob was about a half mile up a side road from Klenke's garage. When Bob knocked on the door, an older man opened it and said, "Guess you're the guy Gus sent our way."

"That's right. Do you have a room?"

"Come on in," the man said.

Moments later, Bob found himself in a small but tidy room. The price was right and the place was clean. He fell back on the bed and sighed with a sense of accomplishment.

"Looks like this whole thing might work out pretty well," he told himself, fending off dark clouds of guilt.

18

"The LORD is my rock and my fortress and my deliverer...."
Psalm 18:2

As Lois and Sandy walked into the kitchen with their shopping bags, their easy laughter was abruptly silenced when they spotted Bob's note on the table. With a sense of unease, Lois picked up the note, reading in disbelief. She crumpled the note, throwing it across the room, as she collapsed into a chair. What had happened to her life? What was she going to do now? Without much emotion, Sandy read the note and tried to convince Lois things would work out somehow. Lois was deaf to her empty words.

She did the only thing she could think of. She picked up the phone and called Al.

"Al, Bob is gone," she said flatly when he answered.

"What are you telling me, Lois?" He was alarmed, thinking she meant Bob was dead!

"He left me, Al. He didn't even say where he was going. He's not coming back ..." She couldn't continue.

"Another Chadwick crisis," Al thought, as he climbed into his car. He felt a rage rising inside him at the pain and damage Bob caused. Now he'd done it again.

* * *

Al found Lois sitting in her kitchen staring out the window, crying, with a half empty cup of coffee in front of her. He pulled up a chair and sat with her quietly for a few minutes. Finally he asked how she was doing.

"I'll be okay," she said, trembling. "Bob will be back and our lives will get back to..." her voice tapered off. "What's he going to do without me?"

She looked up at Al, searching for confirmation. He could tell she didn't really believe what she had just said.

Al felt certain Bob had no intention of coming back. Rather than facing his problems like a man, he had chosen to walk away. There wasn't much he could say to make things less painful for Lois. He cursed Bob under his breath as he drove back home.

*   *   *

At six the next morning, Bob walked into the Viking for breakfast, feeling refreshed after a good night's sleep and a hot shower. He could hear the men's hearty laughs before he came through the door. Spotting Gus, he walked toward the table where four other men were still snorting with laughter.

"Sit down, Bob. Let me introduce you to the boys." Gus was in the habit of taking his breakfast at the Viking most mornings.

"This is, Clarence "Sunny" Sundberg, Charlie Blahnik, Winky Carlson and Howie Krueger."

Bob took a chair and nodded hello. He liked their easy manner. "So, what's the laughing about?"

"Well," Gus began, still chuckling, "Ol' Wink here has a plan. Al Johnson's got a Swedish restaurant down the road in Sister Bay and he's pretty proud of his grass roof. Wink is going to head down there pretty soon and put a few goats up on that roof. Can't wait to hear how that goes over!"

The men laughed heartily again, imagining the surprise on Al's face. When the laughing subsided, Gus told the men how he and Bob had met the night before.

"Bob and I are going to be great friends because he drives a Ford."

Howie, who drove a Ford truck, was a little offended. However, everyone except Bob knew what Gus was insinuating.

"What do you want for breakfast, Bob?" Gus asked, sliding the menu across the table.

"What do you suggest?" Bob asked.

"The bacon and eggs are edible. Joe does the breakfast shift. Not exactly a chef but he can sling food on a grill."

With that, Gus yelled, "Wanda, we're ready to order!" Normally, Bob would feel uncomfortable with the way Gus spoke, but Wanda seemed fine with it. She sauntered over to the table and Bob ordered two eggs, bacon and white toast.

"How do you want your eggs cooked?" she asked.

"On the grill," was Bob's reply.

After a brief silence, the men began to laugh.

"I think Bob's gonna fit in just fine," Charlie nodded.

"We don't let just anyone join us for breakfast, ya know,"

Howie spoke up. "But if you're a friend of Gus, I guess you're okay."

"Wait a minute!" Gus protested. "I've known this guy less than a day and he's already my friend? Maybe we'd better find out if he's a communist, first!"

"Or a queer," Charlie added.

The guys laughed and agreed they'd give Bob a couple of weeks to prove he was republican, straight and not afraid of hard work. They already knew he could handle Joe's cooking.

"So, Bob, tell the boys a little about yourself," Gus suggested.

"Well, I'm originally from West Virginia but moved to Ohio for work. I was hurt in an accident at the steel mill where I worked and couldn't go back. I've been looking for a place to retire where I can fish and enjoy the four seasons. I'm not much of a social person but I like having a couple of good friends."

"Well, there aren't many people in Ellison Bay, so you should be fine," the men agreed.

The conversation flowed and eventually breakfast arrived. The eggs were hard and the toast was burned. The bacon looked barely cooked.

"Wow, Joe did it right for you today, Bob," Gus observed, as the men broke out in laughter again.

"Don't worry," Wink said. "If the food kills ya, we'll make sure you get a nice funeral!"

After the laughter died, Bob asked a serious question.

"Where can a man find a job around here?"

"Can you cook?" Charlie asked? The men snickered again and Bob joined in.

"Seriously," Bob said, "I am going to need a job. Any suggestions?"

"Well," Sunny said, scratching his head, "There are a few commercial fishing operations around here. You know much about fishing?"

That got Bob's attention. "I love to fish," he said. "Used to fish in Sandusky Bay every chance I got."

"I heard one captain needs another guy to help out. Know anything about bait?"

Bob thought for a bit. "Depends. What kind of fish do they go after? What would the job include?"

"They need someone to be in charge of putting the bait on the poles. It's a slimy job. The ad said they were looking for a *master baiter*," Sunny said, slapping his knee.

The men guffawed. Bob had fallen for the bait and they loved it. Bob joined in. Finally he said, "Come on, do you guys know of any jobs around here?"

"This is a small town," Gus said, thoughtfully. "Most folks around here work in a family business or find jobs down in Sister Bay. Some guys even drive to Sturgeon Bay when the shipyard is hiring. There might be work in the fishing industry, but it's seasonal. I have a buddy with a commercial fishing boat. If he needs someone it would be early morning and long days, May through October."

"That would be fine. I'm used to getting up early. What's his name?"

"Let me make a call and I'll let you know tomorrow. Until then, enjoy your breakfast."

Bob smiled, hopeful something might come through for him. Looking around the restaurant, he noticed Timothy Czeck wasn't there. "No Timothy today?" he asked.

"He went to the dentist in Green Bay to have a few teeth pulled." Howie said. "He'll probably be back in tomorrow."

Continuing to gaze around the room, Bob noticed several older couples, but one individual stood out.

"Who is the guy with the long hair?" he asked.

"Oh, that's John Vanderhof," Gus said. "Everyone calls him Van. He used to be known as Door County's resident druggie. Spent a lot of nights in the county jail in Sturgeon Bay. Went to Woodstock in '69 to hear Jimmy Hendrix and Cream and all that heavy stuff, but somehow while he was there he got religion. He calls himself a Jesus freak. He was a little nutsy before but now he's really crazy. Some people around here wish he'd go back to his drugs!"

As Gus was talking about Van, Bob couldn't help thinking about Big Al and Reverend Rico. Then the thought of Joey hit his gut like a boulder. Was it fear? Dread? He had no peace, wondering about his son. Was there more than this life? His thoughts spiraled down and Bob shook his head. He needed to move on.

"So where do you guys get groceries and stuff around here?"

"Right next door," Gus offered. "The Pioneer Store has most everything you need. If they don't, you'll have to make a trip down to Sturgeon Bay or Green Bay."

"Next door sounds good," Bob said, thinking he didn't need much for now. His bigger question was finding a place to stay.

"Any of you know of a place I could rent? Nothing fancy." Sunny spoke up.

"I just might know a place. My mother has a finished basement she's looking to rent. It's got a sitting room with a kitchenette, a bedroom, bath and a private entrance. It's not too far out of town. I've been telling her it would be good to have a man downstairs in case she ever needs help."

"Sounds interesting," Bob said.

"I'll talk to her this afternoon and let you know tomorrow morning at breakfast," he promised. "I'd rather she rent to someone like you than some drunken kids throwing wild parties!" When they got up to leave, they each dropped money on the counter.

"We're on the honor system here, Bob," Charlie explained. "Don't cheat. Leave at least an eight percent tip. If you cheat, you lose a testicle. If you cheat twice, you *eat* the other one!" Bob saw the twinkle in his eye. There was a final laugh as the men left for their workday. All except Bob, that is.

*   *   *

Bob wandered over to the Pioneer store. It was a general store with the usual assortment of produce, dry goods, personal supplies and trinkets. The selection wasn't great and neither were the prices. Bob picked up a local paper, some chips and a coke from the fountain in the back. After paying the clerk, he jumped in his car to take a look around the Ellison Bay area.

The roads were a bit confusing at first. They were not laid out in the one-mile grid pattern like Ohio's familiar farmland. The roads wound through forests of fragrant evergreens and hardwoods, orchards and pastures. It seemed every road led towards water. The coastline varied from bluff to a stony beach. He enjoyed the cool autumn weather and the hint of color in the trees.

He stopped in a park and got out to take in the view. A path led to the edge of the bluff overlooking the water. He watched a few sailboats skim across the bay and a huge freighter making its way north. He looked through the paper and scanned the want ads for jobs. *This is going to be a great place to settle down*, he thought.

Glancing at his watch, Bob was surprised to see it was already late afternoon. He hadn't realized how long he had lingered. On the way back through Ellison Bay he stopped by the Pioneer Store once again, picking up a loaf of bread, a package of bologna and a jar of mustard.

He was ready to enjoy a man's meal and a restful night, but that night was far from restful.

JERRY PRICE & TOM ROY

19

"If we find ourselves with a desire that nothing in this world can satisfy, the most probable explanation is that we were made for another world."
C.S. Lewis

Bob tossed and turned all night. *Must have been the bologna*, he thought, recalling several trips to the toilet. The little sleep he had was filled with a strange nightmare of a two-story bottle of Schlitz chasing him with a knife. Day two in Ellison Bay was not getting off to a good start.

After a quick shower and shave, he dressed and headed to the Viking. Even though he walked through the door by six, he noticed his new friends already seated at the table. Pulling up a chair, he turned toward the kitchen, calling out, "Gimme a Joe Special!"

The waitress raised her eyebrows but he ignored her and turned back to the table. "How're you guys doing this morning?"

That's when Bob noticed the table was unusually quiet. The usual chatter was missing and the mood was glum. Finally Sunny said, "Howie had to put down his dog last night."

"Sorry to hear that, Howie" Bob said. "Anything I can do for you?"

You can shut your damn mouth!" Howie started to get up. "Come on, Howie," Gus said. "I know it's tough but give this guy a break. He didn't know."

"You can shut up, too, Gus!" Howie stormed out. Everyone could see he was taking this hard.

"Let's give him a few days," Gus suggested, and they all nodded in agreement.

There was a moment of silence before Gus spoke up. "Got some good news for you, Bob. My buddy wants to meet you about that fishing job. How about tomorrow afternoon at two?"

"Great!" Bob was very interested. "Thanks, Gus!"

"Oh, yeah," Sunny cut in, "My mother said she might consider renting to ya. Wanna meet her?"

"Sure do!" What had started out as a tough morning was turning into a pretty good day.

The conversation around the table settled into the normal topics. Nothing deep. Just a lot of bull.

*   *   *

The men finished their breakfast and left Bob at the table to choke down the *Special* consisting of two runny eggs and a slice of jerky that vaguely resembled ham. Eventually, he finished and looked around the restaurant. Timothy Czek was walking toward him.

"Sloopy lives in a very bad part of town," he whispered when he got close to Bob.

This was a slam-dunk for Bob. The song had played several times on the radio while he was driving north. He knew it was the Hang on Sloopy by the McCoys, but he would wait until he was ready to leave to give the answer.

As Bob watched Timothy slowly return to his table, he noticed John Vanderhof sitting alone at a back table. He had a book with him and was writing intently on a tablet. There was something intriguing about the guy. Though he was nothing like Big Al, there was something about him that reminded him of his old friend back in Ohio.

What the heck, thought Bob, *I've got several hours to spare.* He walked over to the back table and introduced himself.

"Hi, I am Bob Chadwick. The guys tell me you like to read the Bible. I've read a little bit of it, myself."

"Hey, man, pull up a seat." The man's face lit up. "Name's John, but call me Van. I'm doing a little reading in Philippians. It's a cool book!"

Bob didn't really know what to say, so he blurted out, "I like First Peter, myself."

Van was floored. Was there really someone in Ellison Bay who liked to read the Bible?

"No way! Very cool!" Van said. "Please, sit down." "Sure," Bob said.

The conversation was awkward at first, since Van obviously knew much more about the Bible than Bob did. Fortunately, he didn't stop talking and it gave Bob a chance to gather his thoughts.

When Van stopped to take a breath, Bob jumped in.

"Here's a question for you," he began. "Everyone has a different opinion on what happens after we die. What's your take?"

Obviously, this question still burned deep in Bob's soul. He couldn't stop wondering about his son's death and the hereafter.

"Knock me out, man!" *This guy is going deep right out of the chute,* Van thought. "What if I share my story with you before I answer that?"

Van had plenty to say and Bob had plenty of time, so he agreed.

This should be one interesting story!

JERRY PRICE & TOM ROY

*   *   *

"I used to be a big druggy," he began. "Pot, LSD, the occasional hit of cocaine. Music was my thing, especially Jimmy Hendrix, so I decided to make my way out to the Woodstock music festival in upstate New York. You know about that?"

Was there anyone in America who hadn't heard about it? Drugs, hippies, rock and roll, naked girls and 'free love.'

"Sure, I've heard of it."

"I hitchhiked the whole way. Man, that was a trip! Spent a night sleeping in a hog barn in Indiana. But I made it and the place was amazing. There were thousands of people, as far as you could see, and cars parked for miles along the country roads. It was all about *anything goes*, man! Do whatever you wanna do!

As soon as I got through the fence—I didn't wanna pay— some guy gave me a toke on his weed. Then someone else doled out a bunch of pills. I took some. Heck, they were free! It rained but no one cared.

Before I knew it, I was naked in the mud with a bunch of chicks. Couldn't hide my *emotions*, if you know what I mean. The music kept playing and the drugs kept coming. I don't remember much else, other than the music stopped and the concert was over.

Oh yeah, I remember Jimmy Hendrix playing the national anthem. It was *way* cool. But that's about all I remember. I needed to get back to Door. Kinda tough to hitchhike half way across the country without any clothes!

There was a lake nearby and I washed off most of the mud. I saw a dress on a rock near the lake, so I put it on. Man, those things are comfortable! This one must have belonged to Mamma Cass! It was big and loose.

The first guy to give me a ride was driving a '64 Ford. I can't imagine what he was thinking and I was surprised he stopped. Always wanted one of them Fords! A ways down the road he turned toward me and asked me what I had under that lovely dress. I was still pretty stoned but I smacked him.

He slammed on the brakes, I got out and he tore off. After a couple miles of walking, finally this chick stopped and offered me a ride. She asked where I was going. "*Wisconsin*," I said.

"Jump in," she said. "I'm headed for Chicago."

"I jumped in. What I remember is she smelled great and had long blonde hair. I didn't know what to say so she broke the silence. "I think I have that same dress in my closet."

"Really?" I wasn't sure if she was serious and didn't know what else to say. She smiled and drove on. Eventually I began telling her about Woodstock and why I was wearing a dress. She seemed okay with that.

Turns out, this chick was from upstate New York and had just graduated from college. She was going to Chicago for a job interview and felt she had a pretty good chance of getting the job.

"So you're a college grad?" I asked, impressed.

"Yes, I went to a small college just outside New York City called The Kings College." I asked what kind of school was called the Kings. "It's a small Christian college for kids who want a liberal arts degree with a Bible background," she explained.

"So you're one of those 'we hate sinners' people?" I was trying to be funny.

"Not really, she answered. By the way, my name is Barb. What is yours?'

"You can call me Van, I said. And I've broken every one of the Ten Commandments, so you can let me out now if you want." I was pretty uncomfortable and kinda wished she would.

"Barb laughed and said, "I've broken a few, myself."

I didn't know what to say. I thought all Christians were perfect little goody- goodies.

For most of the way, Barb shared how she had come from a family with a lot of money, but at age fourteen she had rebelled and left home for a few days, eventually coming back.

"My dad and I didn't get along. He was ex-military. Mom was very quiet and never questioned anything dad said or did. My home was definitely dysfunctional," she said.

"One day some kids invited me to a church for a volleyball game. It was fun. I met some new people and our team actually won. Afterwards this guy stood up and started talking about Jesus. He wasn't all religious or weird. In fact, he was pretty cool. He talked about how Jesus is the way to get to heaven."

"Barb went on to say that was the day she decided to give her life to Christ. She went on to explain how Jesus changed her whole outlook on life and how she eventually ended up at The Kings College.

"That's far out!" I said. "That Jesus guy reminds me a lot of Donovan, with the white robe and all."

"She smiled. "Jesus is more than that. When we get to Chicago I'll give you a book to read."

"That's cool," I said.

"Bob, that's all I remember from the conversation. I fell asleep and woke up in downtown Chicago. I had no idea where I was going to stay or what I was going to eat. I had never been to Chicago."

"Barb could tell I was a little lost so she took me to a place called the Pacific Garden Mission. She said that if I listened to their little speech they would give me a meal and a free bed for the night. Free was my kind of language. They sounded like my kind of people.

"When she dropped me off, an old guy introduced himself and asked me a few questions. Then he said, "Let's see if we have some men's clothes for you to wear."

"Free clothes?" I thought. This place keeps getting better. He found some jeans, a flannel shirt, underwear, socks and even shoes that fit. Nothing matched and it was cool. I was glad to donate the dress!

"He led me down a hallway to a room with four beds. Three of them had belongings on them so I figured the fourth one was for me. He handed me a pillow and told me to head down to the chapel in fifteen minutes. I had no idea where that was, but I dressed and followed the others. A bell rang and I found a seat.

This place is full of winos, I thought. "I was surrounded by old guys that looked like they'd been sleeping on the street. The room stunk like pee. I knew some of them were addicts. You know, Bob, a druggie can spot another addict.

Some old chick started playing music on the organ, and it wasn't Rock n Roll on a Hammond B3! Then a bald guy in a suit stood up and began speaking. I wondered if he knew Barb because he talked about the same Jesus stuff.

I remember him saying we are *all* sinners. *Even people like Barb?* I thought. He said all of us, not just the ones in this room, need Jesus. He included himself. He talked about a God who loves us, not an angry God who hates us. He said that's why God sent Jesus, because we all need a Savior.

He explained how Jesus' death made it possible for me to have a new life if I believed. That day turned my world upside down. I'd never heard this before. Could this stuff be real?

When he finished, he asked if anyone wanted to begin a relationship with Jesus. I can't explain it, but I felt this powerful desire in me to have what he was talking about. It was almost as if a force outside me pulled me out of my chair.

A guy came over and sat down beside me. He began to talk about some of the same things Barb had said, but he showed me in the Bible where it said the same thing. The words about jumped off the page!

All of a sudden something broke in me and I started crying. I got it! It all made sense and I understood what I needed to do. Right there I said a prayer and asked for God to forgive everything I had done. I told him I needed him."

I can't explain it, Bob, but I felt lighter, happier...*free!* I went to Woodstock to feel free and left stoned. I came to this mission house and that's where I felt truly free!

The guy prayed for me and asked me if I had a Bible. I told him I did. The book Barb had given me was a Gideon Bible. He suggested I read the book of John. That's my real name so I knew I could remember it. I gotta tell you, I haven't stopped reading that book ever since that day!

Now wait 'til you hear this! One of the guys that worked at the mission was headed to Green Bay the next morning and gave me a ride all the way to Packer land. Pretty cool, huh? I hitch hiked the rest of the way home and when I got to Ellison Bay I was a new man. At first I felt like a fish out of water. Everyone here knew me as a druggie. Now they call me a Jesus freak. They didn't know how to take me.

You know, the church I went to as a kid taught me that God expected me to be a good person. But now I know none of us are good enough. We all need Jesus. I'm just trying to follow him. Eventually I met a man in Ephraim who's the pastor of a small group of people who meet in a home. I hang out with him a lot and he's helped me.

People around here think I'm a freak but I just try to love them. Know what I mean?"

Van stopped and Bob shook his head. The truth was, he had no idea how to love anyone.

"So what's your story?" Van asked. "When did you become a Christian?"

"Well, to be honest," Bob began, "I've read a bit of the Bible and I've gone to church, but I'm not really there yet. It's a long story." Glancing at his watch, Bob saw it was now past noon and he needed to get ready for his interview. At least, that's what he told Van.

"No problem, man. Let's talk more down the road."

"Sure," Bob said, heading for the door. "Thanks for your time."

*   *   *

Bob went back to his room, ate another bologna sandwich and took a short nap. He headed for Gills Rock and waited. He wasn't sure why a job interview would take place at two in the afternoon until he arrived at the dock. The boat was just coming in. It had been out since dawn and the crew was taking out their nets. The captain stepped on the dock and lit a cigar. He was in his mid-fifties but a life on the lake had weathered and aged him.

"You must be Captain Kurt. I'm Bob Chadwick."

The captain turned toward him, took the cigar out of his mouth and spit in the water.

"So? What do you want?"

"Well...I'm here about a job. Gus Klenke tells me that you might have an opening."

"That son of a b****!" he growled. "I never listen to him."

Putting the cigar back in his mouth, the captain walked to the end of the dock. Bob was dumbfounded. Had he made this trip for no purpose at all?

Suddenly the captain turned around and said, "Come on out here! I want to talk to you."

When Bob got to the end of the pier, the captain said, "You see all that water out there?"

"Yeah," Bob replied, "I've spent a good part of my life fishing."

The captain spit again. "You wanna work on a dirty old boat out on rough water like this?"

"I love fishing. I love water and I'm not afraid of hard work." "This is commercial fishing. No bobbers here. It's hard work.

Pay's not great. Be here no later than 4:30 every morning, no matter what kind of weather!"

Bob had to think for a moment. Was he offering him the job? "I need a job and like I said, I'm not afraid of hard work. I used to work in a steel mill. I'll be here at 4:30 sharp." Bob purposely omitted any mention of his disability.

Captain Kurt removed his cigar once more to spit and said, "If you're willing to get paid in cash, I'll give you a chance. The first week you'll get the minimum until I see how you do."

"See you in the morning," Bob said, and they shook hands.

I think I just got a job, he thought, as he headed for his car. He hadn't experienced too many job interviews, but he was fairly sure this one was pretty unique. A handshake with a crusty old sailor was all it took. Bob knew he would make far less money than he had before, but he needed a job.

JERRY PRICE & TOM ROY

* * *

That next morning Bob got up early and drove to the dock, arriving at 4:29 am.

"Where the hell you been?" Captain Kurt shouted at him. "I thought we started at 4:30," Bob answered, surprised.

"Ever heard of Vince Lombardi? You're in Packer country, son.

If you're not fifteen minutes early, you're late. Get your ass on the boat and let's get going. We got fish to catch."

Twelve hours later, with a boat full of fish, they pulled into dock. What a first day! Bob's back was aching, his hands were blistered and bleeding and he really questioned whether this was something he could do for a living.

As he climbed slowly into his car, Bob checked his watch. He had told Sunny he would stop out to look at his mother's house. He pulled off to the side of the road and took a Door County map out of the glove compartment that he purchased at the Pioneer store. Fifteen minutes later he pulled into the driveway of 5223 Twin Pines Drive.

Bob got out of the car and stretched his sore muscles. An elderly woman answered the doorbell on the second ring, looking at him through the screen door. She looked frail and fearful.

"Can I help you?" she asked.

"Mrs. Sundberg? I'm here because Sunny said you might have a room for rent in your basement. Is that true?"

The woman looked Bob over and wrinkled her nose. "What's that smell? Something smells like a dead fish!"

Bob chuckled. "I'm sorry, ma'am. I've been out on a fishing boat and I just got off work. But I promise to shower every day and keep the place clean. I can pay in cash In fact, I'll give you a deposit today if the place works out."

She seemed to relax slightly.

"Well, I don't want you coming in my house smelling like that. If you want to clean up, you can bring my son when you come back. I don't let strange men in my house, anyway. I do read the newspapers, you know!"

Bob had to hide his reaction. The last thing he wanted was to get personal with this old lady!

"I understand. How about if we come by around seven tomorrow night, after I've had time to clean up and grab some supper?"

"I guess, if you bring my son with you." Sunny's mother was no- nonsense.

"I will. Nice meeting you and I'll see you tomorrow at seven," Bob said, as she closed the door.

Bob's aches and pains followed him to bed that night.

20

Hard work beats talent when talent doesn't work hard.
Anonymous

The first few weeks on the job were rough for Bob. When Captain Kurt fished in deep water, they started out before dawn to lift the nets they had set the day before. They would go out about three hours from shore and return mid- afternoon. It was hard work.

Sometimes Kurt made a living from it and sometimes he barely scraped by. And every fisherman knew the lake could claim a life. Everyone remembered Torkel Knutson, who drowned in the waters of Green Bay in June of 1896 when he was 77 years old.

Commercial fishing in Door County has been called *the last of the hunting professions*, and it requires a special type of individual and a dedication to a lifestyle that can be both rewarding and challenging. Kurt had that dedication and Bob was learning. Even though he had worked in a steel mill, this job stretched his understanding of what it meant for him to be a man in the labor force.

Fortunate for Bob, his hands had grown calloused and his muscles had strengthened. Overcoming seasickness was a challenge for all fishermen, but Bob's biggest challenge now was preparing to face the harsh Wisconsin winter, especially in the early morning darkness.

* * *

After successfully negotiating the arrangements with Mrs. Sundberg, by the following evening Bob was comfortable living in her basement. The bed was small, the mattress was old, the bathroom was dated, but everything worked. Just outside his room there was a large wood burning stove, which helped keep the basement warm during chilly autumn nights. He hoped it would perform as well in the deep of winter. The previous April, he was told, dumped thirteen inches of snow in one snowstorm. He was no longer in Ohio.

Because of his job, he could only meet the guys for breakfast on weekends. He missed the daily chatter but he needed the job. The guys seemed to accept him and appreciate that he wasn't afraid of hard work. *Maybe my dad taught me something, after all*, Bob thought. He was especially thankful that his injuries of the past had not hindered him so far. Yes, there was pain, but he had learned to live with it.

* * *

On Saturday morning when Bob walked into the Viking, the table talk was about Wink's prank again. The guys were asking when the goats would appear on the roof of Al Johnson's restaurant.

"You're too busy chasing women!" Howie jabbed Wink in the ribs.

"Nah," Wink shook his head. "Gotta wait til next spring when the tourists come back." Al Johnson was his pal and he wanted to pull his prank when there was an audience. He wanted to make his mark!

* * *

The Pioneer Store was good for basic supplies, but Bob realized he would need to shop for several items they didn't carry. His pay was modest but so was his rent, so he had a little cash set aside for extras. It was time to take a trip down to Sturgeon Bay and load up before winter set in.

When he asked if he could take off work at two the following Friday, Kurt scowled and said nothing. Bob knew Kurt had seen how he worked hard and fought through the pain without complaining.

Finally, Kurt nodded. "Don't expect me to pay you for a full day."

By 2:05 pm, Bob was headed south on Highway 42. He stopped briefly at his place to clean up a bit and less than an hour later he rolled into Sturgeon Bay. With a list of things he needed, Bob began with a stop at H.C. Pranges Department Store. The first item was a fancy electric shaver, on sale for $24.88. He also picked up a bathrobe for $10, even though he'd never worn one before, just in case the old wood burner didn't keep out the winter chill. He had heard the average winter temperatures in Ellison Bay were between zero and 26 degrees, with a record low of minus 27.

He picked up wool socks, a hooded sweatshirt, a pair of lined gloves, a second pair of work boots and a dickie for $4.95. That would do for this trip. He knew he needed a heavy winter coat but that would have to wait. He really wanted to buy an 18"

Emerson tabletop color TV, but with a price tag of $358.00 it would have to wait as well.

After leaving Pranges he headed down Third Avenue to the Bank of Sturgeon Bay, and opened a checking account, depositing $25. His next stop was the grocery store. Spotting Stroh's Pharmacy on the way, he decided to stop there first. There was a flyer advertising free fishing tips. At one time that would have appealed to Bob. Maybe someday it would again. He bought a bottle of aspirin and found a transistor radio for $9.95. That would have to do for entertainment until he could afford the TV.

While he was staying at the rooming house before moving into Mrs. Sundberg's basement, Bob had glanced through a cookbook in the sitting room. The blue cover had caught his attention. It was the 1972 Trinity ALCW Cookbook and inside was a handwritten note by Pastor Paul Sorenson, listing his favorite recipes. Bob had found a scrap of paper and jotted down a few of them, thinking he might get tired of cereal and bologna sandwiches.

He pulled into the parking lot of the Piggly Wiggly, passing Noreen's Shoe Shop on the way but decided to stop there another time. Once inside *The Pig* he began filling his cart. He bought twenty pounds of ground beef at $.57 a pound, eight 16 oz. cans of corn for $.89 each, eight 12 oz. packages of cheese for $.65 each, five 15 oz. cans of pork and beans for $.15 each, two 3 pound cans of Butternut coffee for $2.39 each. In the bread aisle he added eight loaves of *Wonder Bread*, because it *helps build strong bodies 12 ways*! This was all man food. Forget the fancy recipes!

He finished his shopping trip with a 3pound box of Tide soap. Who needed a list? This was all he needed! He paid the checkout clerk and carried his bags to the car.

JERRY PRICE & TOM ROY

*　*　*

It was getting late and Bob was growing hungry, but wanted to see a little more of the town before it got dark. Driving north, he passed the shipyards, amazed at the size of the ships. Several were already docked for the winter. Returning through town, a sign in front of Dick Bosman Ford/Mercury advertised a brand new Ford Maverick for $2150. *Well, I can dream*, he thought.

The Door County Co-op looked like an interesting stop but his growling stomach was demanding to be fed. Back on Highway 42, Bob headed north and stopped at the Road House in Carlsville. Since it was Friday night, the place was packed but he was able to find a small table in a back corner—his favorite spot in any restaurant.

Glancing at a couple next to him, he asked if they recommended anything on the menu.

"Yeah, I recommend you find another place to eat." The man had a full beard and a deep, hearty laugh. His wife giggled.

"Try the perch plate special," the man said.

"Thanks," Bob nodded. "You two from around here?"

The wife answered, "Yes. I'm Pam Folk and this is my husband Gordy. I work for a realtor in Sturgeon Bay and the old man here is a sailor by trade."

"Sailor?" Bob was interested. "What kind of boat?"

"Mostly *Lakers*," he answered. "I work for the Merchant Marines, so I go wherever there's work."

"He's been all over the world but he's home for a few weeks," Pam offered. Gordy just nodded and took a sip of his beer.

The waitress showed up to take their order, but before she could open her pad, Gordy slapped a Twenty Dollar bill on the table and looked up at her.

"Bring us two perch plates and keep the beer coming 'til this runs out. Don't forget your tip!"

Bob chuckled. "Great way to keep the budget in check." The waitress looked over at Bob. "What can I bring you?"

'Guess I'll have the perch plate and a Schlitz."

Remembering his strange nightmare, Bob quickly added, "Wait, make that a Pabst."

Not wanting to bother the couple any more, since Gordy spent so much time away from home, he turned his attention to the other customers. He couldn't help but notice quite a few of the guys wore Green Bay Packer hats. A few had jackets in green and gold. The bar was crowded and every table was full. Bob also noticed the women seemed to be drinking beer right along with the guys.

The food came quickly and fried perch became a favorite of Bob's. He might have to make another trip to Sturgeon Bay soon, with a stop at the Road House.

* * *

As Bob carried his purchases into his basement apartment through the private entrance, he thought he heard a man's footsteps. He wondered if Mrs. Sundberg might have company. Since there was no refrigerator in the basement, the arrangement was that Bob could use the kitchen refrigerator as long as he labeled his own food and didn't touch the rest.

When Bob carried his food upstairs, Sunny was sitting on the sofa. "Hey, Bob, how's it working out down there for ya?"

"Swell," he smiled. "Your mom hasn't kicked me out yet." He was joking but no one else laughed.

"Mom and I have been talking," Sunny began, "and we have a deal for you if you're interested. She tells me you don't have much room for your things downstairs. We were thinking there might be room for a closet if we used some of the space in the furnace room. Nothing fancy. I can pay for the lumber if you can pick it up and build the closet.

Bob didn't have a lot of free time, but he also didn't have anything else to do in the little free time he had. He didn't have a lot of clothes either, but it sure would be nice if they were hung up rather than draped on the chair.

"Where would I go for the lumber?" Bob asked.

"Best bet is the Lily Bay Saw Mill just outside Sturgeon Bay." Bob wished he had known this a day earlier.

"Just got back from Sturgeon Bay, but I guess I could make another trip."

"Great! I'll chip in a couple bucks for your gas," Sunny offered. He jotted down directions to the Saw Mill on a napkin and handed it to Bob.

Bob didn't know it then, but he had just made a date with a bottle of homemade cherry wine.

21

Even if you are a minority of one, the truth is the truth.
Mahatma Gandhi

Bob had his Saturday planned but he didn't want to miss breakfast with the guys. At six a.m. sharp he walked through the door of the Viking and the heckling began. It was good-natured fun and he didn't mind.

"Hey Bob, hope you took a shower! We don't want no stinking *fish* smell around here." Shouted Charlie. Sunny looked down and the other guys roared.

"Hey, how're you and old Kurt getting along?" Winky asked. "Does he have you washing his underwear yet?" The others snickered.

"Hey, it's good to see you, too!" Bob said, looking at each of the guys.

They all laughed. It was a typical day at the restaurant, except this time they had a real cook. Bob ordered 2 eggs, pan fried potatoes and bacon, and it tasted so good he almost ordered another breakfast!

A few minutes later, Gus joined them.

"Hey, Bob," he said, "I heard you and that long haired hippie are best friends now. What's that all about?'

"*Friends* might be a stretch. I asked him about his book and he gave me his life story. Not much else. I just listened."

"Well, be careful. Remember, we told you the guy's nuts. The sheriff thinks he's still doing drugs. Keepin' an eye on him. *No one* can be that happy unless they're *on* something."

"Don't know about that, Gus," Bob said, thoughtful. "I had a friend back in Ohio who was a lot like Van, but without the long hair." "Just be careful, Bob. Don't want you ending up in jail for smoking weed."

"I can take care of myself, Gus."

Timothy Czeck was in the restaurant but as usual he didn't approach the table with others around. Van wasn't there. Probably too early for him.

Bob finished his breakfast and let the guys know he was headed to Sturgeon Bay to pick up some lumber.

"What are you working on?" Howie asked.

"Planning to build a closet off the bedroom." He answered. "Need any help?" Winky asked. Bob was surprised by the offer but before he could answer, Wink added, "Cuz I thought you could ask your long haired friend to help!"

The guys got a good laugh again at Bob's expense, but he took it. He'd fallen for another one of their jokes but he knew they didn't mean any harm.

*   *   *

The Lily Bay Saw Mill was nothing fancy. In fact, it was just a small, open-sided shed with a large circular saw blade. Bob didn't see anyone around but he noticed several trucks parked in front of an old building in the back. Above a sliding barn door was a hand lettered sign that read *Lily Bay Social Club*. A collection of antlers decorated the front of the building.

Bob was greeted by a half dozen of men when he walked inside. It was a workshop with low ceilings and a wood burning stove in the back. There was a layer of sawdust on every surface. Logs were upended for chairs and the room was warm and full of laughter.

A middle aged bear of a man turned and looked at Bob. He was a big man with a barrel chest, calloused hands and a kind face. He stood with his feet apart and his thumbs in his waistband. "What can we do for ya?"

"I was told this was a good place to buy some lumber."

"Might be able to help you out," he said, extending his hand.

"Name's Ralph.

"After shaking hands, Ralph handed Bob a paper cup with what looked like red Kool-Aid. Bob took a sip and raised his eyebrows. The men laughed and told him it was their cherry wine. Each summer several of them went to the orchard and gathered the cherries that fell on the ground. They made their own fermented brew right there at the sawmill which they aged in barrels in the back. It was strong and sweet and went down easy.

"How much lumber will you be needin'," Ralph asked, as he refilled Bob's cup. Bob noticed an assortment of *man* food on the worktable. There was smoked whitefish, saltines, fried fish gizzards and liver sausage. There was a yellow lab named Lily with one of the men and she was happy to clean up any food that fell on the floor.

"Help yourself," someone said, noticing where Bob was looking. "Thanks," Bob said, reaching for a cracker. He needed something to soak up the wine. He was already feeling the buzz. He showed Ralph a rough sketch of the closet he was planning, with some measurements. Ralph did some figuring on a scrap of wood and gave Bob a number. Someone wearing a Yankees cap refilled his cup.

JERRY PRICE & TOM ROY

"We work til around 10 on Saturdays," Ralph grinned. "Then it's social time."

"Sit down," another man said, pointing to an empty log.

Grateful, Bob sat, not sure he could stand much longer. He listened to the happy chatter as his head kept spinning.

"What is this stuff?" Bob asked. "About 20 proof?"

"Nah," one of the men answered. "More like 8 percent." Bob was convinced it was at least twice that much. Noticing Bob was looking for a place to throw out his empty cup, the man said, "Just throw it in the dishwasher."

Bob looked puzzled and the men laughed and pointed at the wood stove. Bob laughed along. He liked this crew!

When he felt steady enough to stand, Bob asked if they had a men's room. Someone pointed toward the back door. It opened to a field. Bob did his business in the tall grass and returned.

"I think I came to order some lumber," he said, giving his head a shake.

"Sorry, we're closed," Ralph said, with a twinkle in his eye. The men laughed again and Bob sensed the years of comfortable friendship. He felt welcome and included.

"I can pick up the lumber next Saturday if that works for you," Bob offered.

"If you come on Saturday, bring some food with you!" a guy in the back shouted.

Ralph draped his big arm around Bob's shoulder and pushed the scrap of wood toward him. "What's your address?" he asked. "Five dollar delivery charge."

"Deal!" Bob responded. He liked Ralph and felt sure he was a man of his word.

Ralph glanced at the address and said, "Ellison Bay? We usually charge six bucks to deliver that far, but I already told you five, so five it is. We'll deliver the wood Thursday afternoon."

They shook hands and Bob headed for Ellison Bay, hardly remembering the drive. It was time for an afternoon nap!

*   *   *

Bob woke up hungry and headed for the Viking Grill, knowing exactly what he would have for supper. The fish boil at the Viking was legendary and it was the only thing on the menu on Saturday nights.

When he arrived there was a large wood fire already going out back behind the restaurant. Locals were gathering, seated on logs. A couple of men carried out a large cast iron kettle, which they set over the fire and filled with salted water. When the water began to boil, they added potatoes, whole onions, and finally fresh whitefish caught that morning. Everything was carefully timed. At just the right moment, one of the men threw kerosene on the fire and jumped back.

The fire leaped into the sky in a spectacular show, causing the kettle to boil over and remove the excess fat from the fish. Using heavy mitts, the men slid wooden poles through the handles on the kettle and carried it into the kitchen. The crowd moved inside and the plates were served. There were steaming chunks of whitefish with the potatoes and onions, all bathed in drawn butter. Each meal came with house made coleslaw and buttered rye bread. Dessert was a slice of delicious Door County cherry pie.

Bob ate alone, but just as he was finishing, Van walked in and spotted Bob in the back corner.

"Hey, Van, how're you doing?" Bob asked.

Van pulled up a chair without an invitation. "I'm doing great, man!" he said. "Had a good time reading the *Word* today."

Bob knew he was in for a long conversation. Deciding he needed to give the discussion some direction, he asked, "Have you thought about my question? The one about what happens to people when they die?"

"Yeah, man." Van said. "In fact I spent all day looking up stuff. I took some notes, too. I have them right here if you want to look at them." Van reached into a well-worn knapsack sitting at his feet.

Bob pushed his chair back from the table and settled in for a long night.

"Hope you can read my writing," Van said, handing Bob several pages of hand written notes torn from a spiral notebook. Like I told you the other day, I believe in Jesus. A lot of people say they believe in Jesus and call themselves Christians but many of them don't really understand what Jesus taught. Most believe he was a good man and he just wants us to be good people. According to the Bible, there is a heaven and a hell, and Jesus is the way to go to heaven when we die. *"That sounds like something Big Al would say,"* Bob thought.

"We can talk more about that in a minute, but first, here's what I found out about some of the more common beliefs," Van continued. "The Jehovah's Witnesses believe that only 144,000 will live as spirits in heaven. The rest of the righteous live on earth and must obey God perfectly for 1,000 years or face annihilation.

"The Unification Church was founded in 1954 and teaches that after death people go to the spirit world. Members advance by convincing others to follow Sun Myung Moon. They do not believe in a resurrection but they believe everyone, even Satan, will eventually go to heaven.

"Christian Scientists believe death is not real and that heaven and hell are a state of mind. They teach one must just attain 'oneness with God'—whatever that means.

"Jewish people are divided. Some believe there will be a physical resurrection. Those who obey the laws of Moses will live with God forever but the unrighteous will suffer. Other Jews believe this life is all there is. They don't believe in any kind of life after death.

"Hindus believe in reincarnation. That means if they live a good life they will return in a higher station in life. When bad things happen they believe it is payment for bad things they have done in a previous life. It's called Karma.

"Buddhists believe people do not have a soul. However, they believe one's emotions can be reincarnated into another person. They do not believe in heaven or hell but they believe a person, with much effort, can reach a state of *Nirvana*, whatever that means. Blissful nothingness, or something like that.

"Islam believes in the resurrection of the body and a final day of reckoning. Eternal paradise is for those who believe in Islam and follow its rules, eternal hell for *infidels*, or those who do not believe in the teachings of their prophet, Mohammed.

"There are other beliefs, but I ran out of time. I've got some books at home on that stuff if you want to read more about it. Here's the big question; what's true?"

Van paused. "Hey, man, I gotta pee!" He got up and ran toward the men's room. "Be right back."

Bob's head was whirling. He couldn't sort it all out and truthfully, they all sounded dismal to him. He was tempted to get up and leave but couldn't bring himself to do it. He needed some answers. Were heaven and hell real? And if so, where was his son?

The question wouldn't leave him alone.

When Van returned Bob was ready. "So, Van, why do you believe what Jesus says? Why don't you believe any of those other religions?"

"I believe what Jesus says," Van said thoughtfully, "because I know who Jesus is and I trust him." He paused to gather his thoughts.

"You know," Van looked at Bob, "all that other stuff is exactly what you called it – religion. They all seem to have a set of rules to follow in order to have a good afterlife. Believing in Jesus is different. Jesus is a person. He is both God and man and he wants us to know him. There are no rules to follow.

"You talk like he's next door," Bob said.

"Actually, that's pretty close to the truth!" Van lit up. "There's a place in the Bible that says he's standing at the door knocking and if anyone invites him in, he will come in!"

Bob shook his head, trying to clear it. He still had no answer to the question that had haunted him every day since Joey died.

"Here's the deal," Van continued. "God already knows everything we've done, and there's no way we can do enough good stuff to make up for the bad stuff."

Bob shifted in his chair, uncomfortable. He felt exposed. He had hoped he could leave his past behind, but it felt like it had followed him all the way to Ellison Bay!

"Believe me, I've done some pretty stupid stuff!" Van said. Bob felt a little better, even though he didn't really believe Van's days as a druggie compared to his rotten past.

"Thing is, God knows we haven't got a chance in hell of going to heaven. Hey, no pun intended," he said, laughing at his own joke. "So he made a way for us. That's the whole reason for Jesus' death. His death paid for our sin because we couldn't pay for it ourselves. He did it all, man!"

Bob was quiet, thinking.

"Look at this," Van said, pointing to a page in his Bible. This knocked me over when I first read it. It's in the second chapter in the book of Ephesians. It says:

> *For by grace are ye saved through faith; and that not of yourselves: it is the gift of God: Not of works, lest any man should boast. (Eph. 2:8-9 KJV)*

"Keep my notes, Bob. Sorry but I gotta run. Peace and love, man!" Van grabbed his knapsack and was out the door.

*   *   *

It was quiet in Bob's basement apartment. His thoughts were still spinning but something was stirring in him. It was as if he was in a fog and couldn't quite see the path. Then a thought came to him.

He thought about Ralph at the Lilly Bay Saw Mill. Ralph was a man of his word and Bob liked that about him. Van talked about Jesus in the same way. John liked Jesus and believed he was a man of his word, which meant believing the Bible, which John called the *Word*.

Ralph talked about delivering the wood at the price he promised. Jesus talked about delivering heaven at the price of his own life. Bob believed Ralph would deliver on his promise. Van believed Jesus would deliver on his promise.

When the wood was delivered, Bob would have to build the shelves himself. But with Jesus' promise, according to Van, all he had to do was turn from his sin and believe in Jesus, God's promised Savior. Was that what Joey had done?

22

We are all so much together, but we are all dying of loneliness.
Albert Schweitzer

Ralph kept his word. On Thursday afternoon he showed up in person with a stack of lumber in his truck. It was actually a little more than Bob needed, but that was fine. A guy never knew when a little extra building material might come in handy.

In spite of the long drive, Bob began to look for excuses to stop in at the Lily Bay 'social club' on Saturday mornings. He enjoyed the men and felt comfortable with them.

Even though he liked the group at the Viking and didn't mind their jokes, he felt accepted at the mill. Maybe it was the cherry wine, but the humor seemed different. At least he wasn't the butt of the jokes! More than that, he had great respect for Ralph. He was dependable as the seasons and his word was gold.

* * *

November brought the promise of winter. Out on the lake, the colder weather and bitter wind made the job on the fishing boat almost unbearable for Bob. There were days every part of him ached, but he wasn't about to let Captain Kurt know. Bob

Chadwick loved fishing, but this was *work! So much for working just through October!*

He made frequent trips to the Pioneer store to purchase a warmer sweater, another flannel shirt or better gloves. The selection was limited but if they got the job done, who cared?

November meant hunting season in Wisconsin. As opening day approached, it was all the men talked about at the Viking. Bob longed to join them. Setting up in the woods early in the morning and joining in the hunt was something he would love, but he knew there was no way he could get a day off. The fishing season was almost over and they had to be out whenever possible. He hoped the guys would at least offer him some venison jerky!

Sure enough, the last Saturday in November, Timothy Czeck walked into the Viking with a large venison summer sausage.

"Thanks, Timothy! You didn't need to do that."

"Yeah, well, I heard you lived alone," he said. "I thought you might need something for Thanksgiving dinner."

Thanksgiving! It hadn't even occurred to Bob he'd be spending the holidays alone. In fact, he hadn't thought about much of anything, including Lois. A few times he had awakened, realizing he'd been dreaming about their life together. He had pushed the thought away. It was another life and he was moving on.

Timothy leaned toward Bob and quietly said, *"I can't live, if living is without you."*

If Bob hadn't known Timothy and his game, he probably would have punched him! But he had grown used to the man's strange habit. After several minutes of searching his memory, he thought he might have the answer. He got up from the table and called across the room, "It's by Badfinger, off the 1970 album, *No Dice.*"

Timothy broke into a big smile.

* * *

For Bob Chadwick, Christmas was just another day on the calendar. Mrs. Sundberg invited him to join Sunny and his family for dinner on Christmas Eve, but he declined. The holiday passed uneventfully. Bob didn't mind missing Christmas. He actually felt pretty good about the fact he that didn't have to spend hard earned money on useless gifts. Yep, there was a bit of Scrooge in him. The holiday wasn't the same without Joey anyway.

He didn't miss his wife at all, he told himself. Well, he did miss her cooking.

* * *

The weather outside was frightful. Bob sat as close to the stove as possible and looked out the back door at the snow. The snow was already about twelve inches deep and the wind was sculpting it into drifts. He was glad to be off work.

He turned on his transistor radio but all he could get was Christmas music, so he shut it off. No holiday celebrating for Bob Chadwick. It was just a day to rest.

Back in Sandusky, Ohio, it was a different story.

* * *

It was a beautiful winter day in Ohio. Two inches of snow had fallen during the night and the plows had already made their early morning run. The sun was shining and the day was crisp.

JERRY PRICE & TOM ROY

Big Al looked out his window and a smile broke across his face. He loved snow and the way it covered everything with a fresh white blanket. It was a beautiful Christmas morning.

As he finished his breakfast his thoughts were on Lois Chadwick. He hadn't seen her in a few months and wondered how she was doing. Christmas might be especially hard on her. He decided to stop by and check on her.

After cleaning up in the kitchen, Al put on his jacket and drove over to the Chadwick house. He knocked on the door but there was no answer. Puzzled, he knocked again. Where could she have gone on Christmas Day?

Walking around to the back, he tried the kitchen door and it was unlocked. Then, he took a chance and pried the door opened. The house was dark and quiet. Too quiet.

"Lois?" he called. No answer. Stepping inside the door, he turned on the kitchen light and saw her. Al stopped, fearing the worst. He spotted the empty bottle of pills on the kitchen counter and walked over. Bending down, he wrapped his big hand around her wrist, hoping for a pulse. Nothing.

Al lowered his head, feeling like he had let her down. If only he'd checked on her more often. A huge tear rolled down his cheek.

* * *

Bob woke up every morning, went to work and gave little thought to anything about Sandusky, Ohio. He had no idea what was going on with Lois. His only thought was himself.

Although Bob had left Lois months earlier, the reality was that Lois had now left Bob. By taking her life, she was, essentially, giving Bob the finger.

JERRY PRICE & TOM ROY

There was no funeral for Lois. In her loneliness and rejection, Lois had avoided people. She had few friends. Big Al and his brother, Richard, stood at the gravesite. Al wept for Lois and the hopelessness she had felt.

Sandra, the Chadwick's foster daughter, was there as well. She had learned of Lois' death from a neighbor who knew how to reach her. She had moved in with a boyfriend and she knew Lois wasn't happy about it, so they didn't have much contact. Sandra was aware of all the pain Bob had caused his wife. She felt a measure of relief for Lois who was now free from that pain.

Al worked through a local attorney, Roger Stonewall, to handle all the paperwork. Roger was a good man. In addition to his law practice, he had investment properties that he fixed up and rented.

On weekends he often sang in a local rock and roll band. He cared about people, especially those down on their luck. He worked hard to make sure that all the paperwork was done properly.

After paying for the funeral and other miscellaneous expenses, there was just over three thousand dollars in Lois' bank account.

Since Sandra was the only living survivor, Al saw that she received the full amount. He also made sure she would receive Bob's disability checks. It was the least he could do for Lois.

* * *

On April 13, thirteen inches of snow fell on Ellison Bay.

"What the hell!" Bob thought. *"When does spring ever come up here?*

Bob was getting restless. Things were becoming routine, even boring. Should he quit his job? Should he think about moving again? He wouldn't mind a *woman* once in a while! As gusts of snow swirled in the air, so did Bob's mind.

* * *

One Friday night Bob drove to the Sister Bay bowling alley for their perch plate. He noticed a guy wearing a white collar and Bob assumed he was a priest. The man motioned to Bob, "Could I borrow your salt shaker?"

"Sure, Father." Bob handed him the salt.

The man looked up, amused. "You can call me Ben. I'm off work now."

Bob wasn't sure about that but he chuckled and agreed. "How long have you been a priest, Ben?"

"Since I finished seminary. By the way, I didn't get your name." "Oh, I'm sorry. Bob Chadwick."

"Nice to meet you, Bob." I'm the oldest of five kids. It was kind of expected the oldest son become a priest. I went to St. Francis and decided to become a priest in fifth grade."

"So you were always a holy person," Bob said."

"Not at all. In fact, I loved to play guitar and sing. I liked all that wicked ol' rock and roll. I still do. In fact, I'm bringing a few big name bands up to Door County to play at our church youth center. Do you like the Turtles and Young Rascals?"

"No, I'm not really into that kind of music, Ben, but I don't mind it."

Ben nodded. "Okay. Well, if you're not busy, come on over next Friday night and see the Turtles. I'll leave you a ticket."

"Thanks, I'll plan to be there."

"Would you like to know why I plan these concerts on Friday nights?" he asked, with a grin. "It's so busy people like you will stay home on Saturday night and rest so they can make it to mass on Sunday!"

Bob thought Ben seemed like a pretty cool priest and looked forward to the weekend.

When he arrived at the youth center Friday night, kids were everywhere. Most were sitting on the floor. Bob settled in next to a woman who looked to be about ten years younger than he was. She turned to look at him and they locked eyes for a second.

The concert was good and it was a good change of pace for Bob. He found Father Ben and thanked him for the ticket. Ben invited Bob to come back but Bob was not sure he was up for another evening of sitting on the floor.

* * *

On Saturday morning, Bob stopped in at the Pioneer Store for a few supplies. It had become a routine. As he walked down one of the aisles, he caught a glimpse of someone who looked familiar. It was the woman from the concert.

"You were at the concert last night, right?"

"Yes, she said. "You sat right next to me and never said a word." That caught Bob off guard.

"Did you like the group?"

"Well, yes, that's why I went." He thought he saw her roll her eyes.

This was going nowhere fast. After a few more awkward questions, Bob decided he would try one more time.

He asked about her family. Her eyes got moist and she looked away.

JERRY PRICE & TOM ROY

"You ok?"

She was silent. Finally, she said, "My father passed away last week. I'm staying with my mother right now." Bob felt his heart tug a bit.

"I'm sorry."

"He was a wonderful man," she began, but couldn't continue.

Bob was uncomfortable. He wasn't sure what to do. Finally, he said, "Do you need to talk? We could sit in my car where it's more private."

She nodded, still crying. Bob drove toward the lake and found a place to park.

She talked about her father for a few minutes, relating stories of all the ways he helped people. Bob was beginning to feel he had known her father. He reached over and took her hand. Wait! Was he getting soft? That wasn't the Chadwick way. He knew what he wanted and it was more than holding hands.

Before the morning was over, *more* was what he got. He had his own rock and roll event in the back seat. *"What a morning,"* he thought. *"And in broad daylight!"*

"What's your name?" Bob asked? "Beth. What's yours?

"Steve Sanders," he answered. "Do you need a ride home?" "You can drop me off back at the Pioneer Store. My car's there.

Will I see you again, Steve?"

"Sure. I'm sure I'll see you around. This is a small town."

The next morning Bob slept late. No work, no mass, no worries. Just the satisfaction in knowing he still had it.

JERRY PRICE & TOM ROY

23

Spring makes its own statement, so loud and clear that the
gardener seems to be only one of the instruments,
not the composer.
Geoffrey B. Charlesworth

Spring is a time of new beginnings. For Bob, however, it was all
wind, rain and rough water. The bitter winter had left a thick layer of
ice on Lake Michigan and it was slow to break up. Because Door County
is surrounded by water, the slowly melting ice and the wind off the lake
cause spring to be slow in coming. The Great Lakes can be fierce any
time of year, but the ice shoves and sudden changes in weather made
Bob's work on the fishing boat challenging.

It didn't help that Captain Kurt and his shipmate, Brian, were
silent and surly, especially at 4:30 in the morning. He knew the only
reason Kurt didn't fire Brian was because he was a relative. There was
no love between them and they were getting on Bob's last nerve. The
lake was bitter cold but Bob's attitude was even colder.

Even Saturday mornings at the Viking were getting old. Gus had
been a real friend but the others often irritated Bob. In fact, one
morning when Bob was sitting alone at the Viking, he saw Timothy
approaching and told him to take a hike. Timothy just lowered his head
and walked away. No song title that day.

April 18—the date was burned on Bob's brain—was a game
changer. It had been a rough week on the boat, worse than normal.
Brian was lazy, forcing Bob to pick up the slack. He whined and
complained about everything. Bob had nearly snapped. Everything
inside him wanted to heave his lazy ass overboard. Driving home,

he was in a black mood. *"I hate fish!"* he thought. *"And I hate that little jerk, Brian, even more!"*

* * *

After a quick shower, Bob decided against the Viking and drove down Highway 42 into Ephraim to grab a burger at Wilsons. It was pre-tourist season and the place was fairly empty when he arrived.

He ordered a burger basket with fries and sat staring out a window at the bay and the brown bluff across the way. Everything was barren now, but soon the county would come alive. The trees would bud, spring flowers would bloom, shops would open and the tourists, who were the lifeblood of Door County, would come.

Bob was in a dark mood and his thoughts went deeper than usual. *"Why am I here?"* he wondered. *"What am I doing in Door County and why did I think I would be happy fishing for a living?"* He allowed his thoughts to spiral down. *"What the hell am I doing with my life?"* he thought. *"Does it even matter? Is there anything that matters?"*

After downing the burger, Bob still had a hole in his belly. He tried to fill it with two scoops of ice cream but when he was finished, the only thing that felt full was his brain. It was a tangle of thoughts he couldn't sort out and he needed some relief.

Bob had worked hard all winter and had only allowed himself an occasional beer. He had lost weight and felt better. He decided he deserved a mini *vacation*, so he stopped on his way home for a case of Schlitz.

That night he had no idea how many beers he had consumed before falling into a deep sleep.

* * *

Bob had a restless night. A few times in his life he remembered having vivid dreams, but that night his dreams went beyond memorable.

His first dream was of Lois. She was walking down a lane lined with trees and wildflowers. She had a smile on her face and looked truly happy. Suddenly a man appeared. It was Big Al!

Bob could see him moving toward Lois, placing his hands on her waist and kissing her. Bob woke up with a jolt! He felt a rage inside him.

"I knew Al was a fake! He's just like Rev. Rico!" he thought.

Bob calmed down by reminding himself it was only a dream. As he thought about it, he realized it was the first time he had actually felt something for Lois in a long time. He wondered about her. *"I took care of her,"* he told himself, remembering that he had left her his disability income. But that didn't assuage the guilt that nibbled at the edge of his conscience. *"You walked out on your wife,"* his conscience was trying to tell him. *"You left her when she needed you."*

He tried to silence the voice within. Eventually he fell back to sleep.

*   *   *

Bob woke in a cold sweat. He didn't know how long he had slept but the second dream was far more vivid than the last. He remembered every detail. Was it Ellison Bay or Sandusky Bay? He couldn't tell. The street was narrow and everything looked old. He heard voices. It was a crowd and the noise was growing louder.

There was a man carrying a large wooden beam over his shoulder. The man was badly beaten and the crowd was taunting. The man stumbled and fell. A guard commanded a dark skinned man to pick up the beam.

The next scene was gruesome. The man who had been beaten was thrown on top of the beam. Someone took out long iron spikes and began pounding them through the wrists of the man, attaching them to the beam. Bob was in agony. He could feel the pain each time the spike was driven further into the man's flesh. They crossed the man's ankles and drove a spike through both feet. The beam was hoisted upright. The man cried out in excruciating pain. Or maybe it was Bob, himself, crying out.

People were standing around, watching, sneering, and mocking.

JERRY PRICE & TOM ROY

The man tried to lift himself up, gasping for air. Bob was gasping for air. He could barely look.

The dream shifted. The crowd grew, shouting at the dying man. They wanted nothing to do with him. Suddenly Bob knew he was part of that crowd.

A man approached Bob. He felt suddenly guilty, ashamed. But there was no condemnation on the man's face. "Are you ready to stop running, Bob?" "But..." Bob tried to speak.

"I know."

Bob knew, with those two words, the man knew everything about him. He also knew the man had died for *him*.

"Trust me," the man said.

When he woke, Bob was exhausted. "It was just a stupid dream," he told himself. *"It was the beer."* He tried to distance himself from the dream but he couldn't. He was tired. He was tired of running, tired of trying to figure things out. He was tired of himself and his stupid, selfish *Chadwick* pride.

"Trust me," Jesus had said.

Something broke inside Bob. He sat up and cried out loud, "I'm done! I'm tired of running. I give up!" Lowering his head, he said, "Jesus, take over my life."

There was a long silence. Slowly, a peace settled over Bob. His wall of pride began to crumble and he began to weep softly. He wept for the pain in his life. He wept for the people he had hurt. He wept for Jesus and the pain he had endured. He wept with the relief of forgiveness that flooded through him. He wept because he knew he didn't deserve it. He wept with the hope of a new beginning.

*   *   *

Bob jumped out of bed with a new energy. Was this real? Did Jesus really speak to him in a dream? Did he just give Jesus his life? He was afraid to embrace what had just happened.

He knew he needed to talk with someone. It was only five fifteen. Would Van be at the Viking this morning? He hoped so.

When he arrived, he spotted the guys at their usual table, but he waved and walked past them, sitting down with Van across the room. As usual, he was sitting alone with his Bible and a spiral notebook.

"Mind if we talk a minute?" Bob asked as Van looked up.

"Hey, Bob!" Sunny yelled over at him. "What the hell are you doing? We're not good enough for you today?" The men laughed. Bob smiled and nodded.

"What's happening, man?" Van motioned for Bob to sit down. "I need to talk to you," Bob began. "Something really strange happened to me last night."

Van was listening.

Bob began relating the details of the dream. When he was finished, Van said, simply, "Cool!"

"So you don't think I'm crazy?" Bob still didn't know quite what to think about it all. Did Jesus really talk to people in dreams?

Van thought for a minute. Then he looked up at Bob. "God speaks to us through his Word. But the Bible also talks about Jesus speaking to people in dreams. I guess God will do whatever it takes to get our attention."

"I had a friend back in Ohio like you." Bob said. "He used to talk to me about God. He talked about things the Bible says."

"Maybe you've been trying to run from it and the only way Jesus could get you to listen was in a dream," Van suggested. "He had to show you the cross to show you he's not looking to punish you but to forgive you."

John didn't have to say it, but Bob knew he saw right through his pride.

"I told him to take over my life, Van." Bob confessed. "I've screwed it up and I'm tired. Maybe Jesus can sort out the mess I've made."

"You've been looking at religion and what others believe," Van said. "I knew you were looking for answers. Jesus answered your questions by showing you the cross. When you asked him to take over your life, he gave you more than you asked for. When you gave up, he gave you forgiveness. When you gave him your life, he gave you heaven."

Bob choked up and couldn't speak for a moment. Things were coming into focus. Finally he said, "I think I get it. I never really understood the cross before. It didn't make sense. I want to trust Jesus, but I'm scared." He couldn't believe he had admitted that.

"Thanks for being honest," Van said. "So what's next? What do I need to do?"

"You know, people might be tough on you," Van answered, looking over at the table across the room. "Don't be surprised if people push you away."

Bob sensed he was probably right.

"Remember, Jesus doesn't expect us to be perfect. He knows this is all new for you. Begin by reading the Bible each day. It's the way we get to know him and grow in our faith."

"Ok, but how do I know what I should do?"

"He'll show you," Van answered, "one day at a time."

Bob was trying to take it all in. He wondered about the big questions, like what he was supposed to do with his life. Should he join a church? Quit his job? Move again? He felt like he should *do* something. Van was telling him to let God show him. He had so much to learn.

Maybe the best way to sum up what God asks of us is when Jesus said, "Love the Lord your God with all your heart, soul, mind and spirit and love your neighbor as yourself." Van pointed to Matthew 22:37.

As Bob was thinking, Van broke in, "Hey man, I've been down the same road. I'm happy to meet with you every day if you want to read the Bible together. We can start in the book of John."

Bob pushed his chair back. "Thanks. I'll let you know. Right now I'm trying to figure out what to say to the guys at that table over there."

"I hear ya," Van said. "For now, just think about how important you must be for Jesus to show up in your dreams, man! In person!"

Bob paused. "I could meet you on Monday," he offered. "Cool. I'll be here."

Bob made his way over to the table to sit with the guys. "Hey numb nuts," Howie said, "What was that all about?"

"Yeah, you two dating now?" Winky chimed in.

"I'm here for breakfast," Bob answered, motioning to Wanda. "Let me get my order in."

"I think you were ordering some *Mary Jane* over there," Charlie suggested. "You two seemed a little too secretive to be talking about anything else."

Bob leaned in. "We're secret lovers," he whispered. The men laughed out loud. He had gotten over that hurdle but Bob knew navigating his new life with his old friends would not be easy.

* * *

Bob spent the rest of the weekend reading through the book of John. It answered a lot of his questions but he had a thousand more. In spite of his questions, the book seemed to come to life. He had no idea where his life was headed, but the words rang true and he had an underlying sense of peace.

When his alarm sounded at three thirty Monday morning, he had a new attitude. However, on the way to work he began to wonder how he should react to Captain Kurt and Brian. He decided he would be as kind as possible. That seemed safe.

"Morning, Brian." Bob greeted him cheerfully. Brian didn't even look up.

"Hey, about Friday. My fault. Sorry." It just came out! Bob couldn't believe he had just said that! Brian glanced at him. He didn't respond and the boat pulled out from the dock.

Work was the same. The day was long and work was hard.

However, Bob cared about pulling his load, and Captain Kurt noticed. By Thursday he couldn't deny something was different.

"Hey Bob, what's up? "Whaddya mean Charlie?"

"Seems like you like your job better."

"Well, Skip, I'm just enjoying life. I'm a happier man, if that's okay."

"We'll see. One bad day and the old Bob will be the same bitch of a self. Don't really care, long as you get your work done."

Bob decided to take the captain's comment as a compliment as well as a challenge. He continued to work hard.

* * *

It surprised Bob that he looked forward to his time with Van.

Never did he dream he would enjoy meeting with a longhaired hippie Jesus freak to study the Bible! Each time they met, his eyes were opened to something new.

"Bob, when all you have is Jesus, you cling to him." He thought long and hard about that statement.

Whenever Bob had a question, Van seemed to have great insight. He drew from many resources other than the Bible. He often quoted one of his favorite writers, C. S. Lewis. He shared several quotes from *Mere Christianity* on the theme of pride.

> *"If anyone would like to acquire humility, I can. I think tell him the first step. The first step is to realize that one is proud."*
>
> *If you think you are not conceited, it means you are very conceited indeed."*
>
> *"According to Christian teachers, the essential vice, the utmost evil, is Pride."*
>
> *"For pride is spiritual cancer; it eats up the very possibility of love, or contentment, or even common sense."*

Bob began to see that what he thought of as 'the Chadwick way' was nothing but pride. Pride did not make him a man. He felt like he needed to start life over again. He needed to be *re-fathered*.

That's exactly what was happening to Bob, though he didn't realize it at the time.

* * *

God was steadily working in Bob's life. As the weather warmed, so did Bob's soul. It was all because of Jesus and a longhaired freak like Van, who faithfully invested in his life. He was learning that we are all made of the same mud but have been built for relationships, which was a real game changer for a loner like Bob Chadwick.

JERRY PRICE & TOM ROY

Bob still had vivid dreams occasionally, but nothing like his dream about Jesus. He believed God often spoke to him in everyday things, and he saw the fingerprints of God in things like a sunrise, a still, starry night or a chance encounter. He began to look for God in other people, like Captain Kurt and Brian, as well as his friends in Ellison Bay.

Saturday mornings at The Viking were part of Bob's routine. He enjoyed the guys and wanted to be a good influence on them. Even though he prayed on his way in, he often found himself taking part in their gossip and profanity. He felt a tug of guilt when he laughed at their jokes, especially if they were at someone else's expense. He knew he had a lot to learn.

One day as he was thinking about how much he had been forgiven, he began to realize he needed to ask forgiveness from people he had hurt. It wouldn't be easy.

The first person that came to mind was Beth. His actions had been totally selfish. She had been vulnerable and he had used her. He felt sad for the hurt he had caused her. He wondered how to get in touch with her.

He decided to talk to Van about the whole idea of forgiveness.

Of course John had plenty to say, but what stood out to Bob were Jesus' words.

"If you forgive those who sin against you, your heavenly Father will forgive you. But if you refuse to forgive others, your Father will not forgive your sins." Matthew 6:9

Those words cut through Bob like a knife.

"What do I do if I never see the person again?" he asked Van. "How can I ask them to forgive me? What if I don't know how to find them?"

"The Spirit of God brings people to mind," Van said, "people you need to forgive and people you need to ask to forgive you. The first thing you need to do is ask God for his forgiveness if you've hurt someone. He's already promised that to us. There will be some people you will never have the opportunity to ask. People move in an out of our lives. There will be others who won't want to hear it. Our responsibility is to seek forgiveness whenever possible."

Bob listened, taking it in.

"If someone comes to mind you know you've hurt, seek them out. If you aren't given the chance to ask them to forgive you, *you can pray they will not live under the shame you caused them.* If you have the chance, ask the Spirit of God to give you the right words.

"Sometimes people don't respond well. That's not your problem. Leave them in God's hands. Believe me, I've had to ask for forgiveness a lot. I've hurt a lot of people and I feel bad about what I've done. The pain I've caused is real. But so is God's grace. I have to trust that God can work in their lives like he's working in mine.

Bob wondered if he would be able to contact Beth. Van's words were sobering. He realized at some point he would need to return to Sandusky Bay. There were quite a few people there he had hurt. Yet the more he thought about it, the more he dreaded it.

* * *

The next few weeks were a struggle. Captain Kurt noticed some of Bob's good cheer was missing, although he remained cordial and continued to work as hard as usual. Bob was wrestling with the Spirit of God. He knew what he needed to do and he didn't want to do it.

It was obvious something was bothering Bob. When he stopped in at The Viking on Saturday morning, they guys sensed it and eased up on their good-natured abuse.

He continued meeting with Van. Van knew Bob was troubled but didn't press the issue. He knew God was working.

24

"He that drinks his cider alone, let him catch his horse alone."
Benjamin Franklin

As the summer came to a close, Bob made a decision. He needed to return to Sandusky and try to restore his relationship with Lois. He knew he had hurt Al deeply as well. He might even try to talk with their foster girl, but he hadn't made a decision on that one yet.

Bob invited Van over to talk with him about his plans. Van had been aware of Bob's struggle and had prayed for him often. When he heard what Bob planned to do, he was pleased. He believed Bob had sensed this was what God was asking him to do but had resisted.

Finally, it seemed, Bob had surrendered and stopped struggling. "If you believe God is telling you to do this, you need to be obedient. This is important because this is how you learn to trust

God. But I want you to promise me that when you get there, you'll find someone to continue meeting with you. In fact, it would be good if you would find a church to attend. You've just starting learning the Word of God and I don't want you to quit. There's so much more!

Bob agreed, although he wasn't too sure about the church part. "If you return to Sandusky," Van said thoughtfully, "I think you should give Captain Kurt at least a two week notice." He didn't hesitate to give advice since Bob had asked him to do that.

I hadn't thought about that," Bob said, agreeing. "I guess that would be the right thing to do."

Van became strangely quiet. Bob knew he had something on his mind and waited. Finally, he asked, "Bob, may I ask you to pray with me about something?"

Bob was surprised and pleased. "Of course," he answered.

Unfamiliar but pleasant emotions were welling up in him. Six months ago, who would have imagined he would have a friendship with this unusual man. And now, here they were, Van asking *him* to pray. And he, Bob Chadwick, was *happy* to pray for his friend. He truly *cared* about Van, and that was an entirely new emotion for Bob. Van had taught him what it meant to care for someone else, to think about someone other than himself, to be brothers in Christ.

"Thanks, Bob. Something's come up. I've been asking God for direction, sensing he has a purpose for me outside Ellison Bay.

Recently I was asked to join the staff of a kind of men's Christian boot camp in Canada.

"Uncle Joe, a counselor I met at the rescue mission in Green Bay, took a job at a ministry called 2BRealMen on *Root Hog Island,* on the Lake Of Bays. He suggested their board get in touch with me to help him in his work with the men. Their goal is to see men healed and restored. They asked if I would come as a Bible teacher for their staff.

"It's very appealing and it might be God's plan for me. But I'm not sure. I wonder if it's only something *I* want. Or, do I just want to quit my job here? Gotta admit, there are days that working in the sanitation business kinda stink! Especially on a hot summer day!"

Bob chuckled. "Sure, I'll be glad to pray about that. Where is the camp located? What part of Canada?"

"It's in Ontario, about a hundred and seventy miles north of Toronto."

Bob's heart stopped for a second. That would put the camp not too far from Denbigh, which held unbearable memories for him. He had no idea what God was planning, or how he would work through his prayers for his friend.

*   *   *

When Van left, Bob began thinking about his future. Life was complicated. He had done a lot of damage and he needed to face it. When he made the decision to follow Jesus, his life improved. But it wasn't easy! His old habits were deeply rooted.

Slowly, Bob was learning to think about other people rather than just himself. He was learning to take responsibility for his actions rather than blaming others or making excuses. He was learning to relate to others with honesty over manipulation. He was learning to give as well as take and he was finding the value of forgiveness over bitterness. He was learning how to be obedient to the nudges of the Spirit of God. And, he was learning that this was how a real man lived life, which wasn't for the weak!

Armed with the knowledge that it wouldn't be easy, he showed up at the dock Monday morning, ready to face Captain Kurt. After a good day on the water, he asked the captain if he could have a word with him. After they finished unloading the boat they headed for the smokehouse so they could speak privately.

"Captain, I want to tell you how much I appreciate you giving me a chance. I needed the work and I've tried to work hard so you wouldn't regret hiring me. You have a good business going here."

Kurt eyed him suspiciously.

"You've probably noticed that I've changed lately." Kurt nodded slowly.

"I've never told you my background but I need to go back to Ohio and make things right with a few people."

Bob was struggling to continue. Kurt sensed where this was going and wasn't too happy about it.

Finally, Bob spoke. "I walked out on my wife. We lost our son in an accident and she was taking it really hard. She even tried to take her life. After a while I couldn't take it. I just left." When Bob heard himself speak those words out loud, the reality of his selfish, twisted actions hit him hard.

Kurt's face grew dark and Bob could feel his anger.

"I just wrote a note and left!" As Bob spit those words out, he experienced being thoroughly disgusted with himself.

"You're a real son of a bitch!" Kurt snarled. "You're quitting, aren't you? I knew you were a lowlife!"

Bob had prepared himself for Kurt's reaction.

"I'm leaving in couple of weeks. I wanted to give you a few weeks to find someone else."

He took a deep breath. He realized Kurt was one of the people he had hurt and even though he had dreaded talking with him, he wanted to do the right thing.

"You think I can fill this job in two weeks? You'd better stick around until I can hire someone!" Kurt was muttering expletives under his breath.

"I'll do my best, but I really need to head back to Sandusky." Bob knew if he didn't leave soon, he might lose the will to go.

JERRY PRICE & TOM ROY

"Everything in me wants to kick your sorry ass out of my sight!" Kurt wasn't happy about Bob leaving, but there wasn't much he could do about it. He began to calm down a bit.

"I gotta admit," he said, "most guys I've hired just quit showing up. At least you had the balls to tell me you were leaving."

"I'm sorry, Kurt."

"Don't think you can slack off just because you're leaving," Kurt added. "I expect you to get your work done." Bob understood.

Reluctantly, Kurt shook Bob's hand as they parted. The sense of relief Bob had to get this conversation behind him was freeing. He knew he'd done the right thing but he also admitted, *I'm looking forward to being free of smelling like fish!*

* * *

Breakfast at the Viking on Saturday morning was the usual. Along with bacon and eggs there was the usual assortment of bad language, bad jokes and loud bodily noises. Bob waited for a good time to bring it up, finally just blurting it out.

"Hey guys, I'm going to be heading back to Ohio." "What the hell!" Sunny said.

"You going to Bible school or something?" Charlie asked. "You've been hanging out with that Bible freak." The rest snickered.

"No." Bob answered slowly. "I've never told you guys the truth about me." He gave them the short version of his previous life.

The men listened and grew quiet. Gus broke the silence.

"Well, there goes that new boat I was planning on buying. When I saw that old Ford and knew I'd be making some good money off it."

The guys laughed, easing the tension a bit. The unspoken thought on all their minds was how Bob wasn't really one of them anyway. He wasn't a native. And no matter how long he lived there, he'd never really be one of them.

"Well, you're like all the rest, Bob." Winky said. "People leave." "Our kids don't stick around either," Howie added. "So when are you leaving, Bob?"

"In a couple of weeks."

Sunny jumped in. "Make sure you let my mom know. She depends on that rent money."

Bob felt sad about leaving Mrs. Sundberg. Her health was declining and he knew she needed someone around. "I'll be sure to tell her."

Sunny was the first to get up from the table. The others followed.

"I guess we'll have to buy your breakfast next week," Gus said.

He was a kind man and it was a gesture of good will.

"Thanks," Bob said, "but it's not necessary." He wouldn't leave without saying goodbye to the guys.

* * *

Most men are not good at saying goodbye. Bob stopped in for his last breakfast at the Viking and the conversation was uneasy. The breakfast, however, was classic. The chef served scrambled eggs and venison sausage with a side of leftover whitefish from the fish boil the night before. Everything tasted like fish. After breakfast the guys each ordered a scoop of ice cream to kill the fish taste. Gus picked up the check.

"A breakfast I'll never forget!" Bob said. They all laughed and shook hands.

Before leaving, Bob felt the need to tell the guys what they meant to him.

"You guys have no idea how much I appreciate your friendship. When I arrived I was a mess. I was lost and lonely and you made me feel like one of you. I'm not good at speeches but I just wanted to say thank you."

"Okay, now get the hell out of here!" Gus said, trying to lighten the moment.

"See ya," Bob said, as he headed out the door. They all knew they'd probably never see him again. He had already said so long to Van.

After saying goodbye to Mrs. Sundberg, someone he'd grown fond of, Bob stared at his new closet as he packed. *"I'm gonna miss this place,"* he thought. *"But I gotta do what's right."*

Next stop, Sandusky, Ohio.

* * *

Leaving Door County behind him, part of Bob was looking forward to seeing Lois and asking her forgiveness. And, he wondered if there was a chance of them ever being happy together.

There was a battle inside him and he knew it was between his conscience and a desire to revert to his old ways. He knew the choice was between following God or the evil one. And he knew he would be in this battle the rest of his life.

JERRY PRICE & TOM ROY

What he didn't know about was the battle facing him in Sandusky, Ohio.

UPSHOTS

Bob Chadwick has to deal with moments of being alone in his own proverbial *woods*, where the decision to be a man or remain in *boyhood* is frequently at hand. Where the consequences of making choices are inescapable. His life journey began being born another man's son through no doing of his. But the path Bob takes into manhood will be on him.

Will Bob's family of origin, his peer groups, the guys he's hung with, or having Budweisers and living in secrecy be the measure of manhood? Will he reach deeper into a responsible love, when being alone *in the woods* is unavoidable? Where Bob's resolve is not to live in duplicity but to love others with accountability.

How much can Bob take? His life has been stranger than fiction. What will he do when he discovers Lois is gone? It's only been since mid June of 1973 that Joey died and now, he faces yet another tragedy slightly over one year later.

Amazingly, Bob does come away from Door County with a new heart and begins to sprout a new mind. Will it be enough to deal with the wounds he'll have after he returns to Sandusky Bay?

One thing is for sure. No man can do life alone, even though our manhood can grow exponentially greater when we face our own woods of uncertainty head on. Not knowing what's around the corner.

JERRY PRICE & TOM ROY

Of all places, the **Lake of Bays** On Root Hog Island in Ontario, Canada will bring the healing Bob needs and wants. Look for him in the coming book of this trilogy to see the change. Where a man becomes a man in the deeper parts of soul and spirit.

- Jerry Price MA
Professional Counselor/Consultant Author of
Transforming Twisted Thinking
Co-Author with Tom Roy of Sandusky Bay and Ellison Bay
Founder Of MORE Married Conferences Co-Founder of 2BRealMen Initiative

Annotations

Winky Carlson pulled off his practical joke of putting goats on the roof of his friend's restaurant. In the process, he fell and broke his leg, so in a way, the joke was on him. However, to this day the tourists still stop to stare at the goats on the grass roof of Al Johnson's restaurant in Sister Bay.

*   *   *

As you traveled with Bob through Door County, WI, the places mentioned are real. It's a beautiful peninsula well worth visiting for its wonderful people and rich cultural experiences.

In Chapter 9 the following statement was made: "In the summer 1961 the Viking held and served their first Fish Boil. Fish boils had their roots in a traditional Potawatomi feast." Some folks may believe the fish boil originated in the logging camps in Door County. The following historical account was taken from the Door County Almanak No. 3 on pg 25 from the Dragonsbreath Press, Sister Bay, WI.

"It is fitting that any historical account of earliest fishing in these Upper Great Lakes should at least mention the efforts of the Native Americans; and because these natives left no written records, such mentions must come from the French. So we learn from the Baron de Lahontan that the Potawatomi of the Door County region were familiar with a delicacy well-advertised today: In the 1680's the Baron observed a four-course feast which began with "two whitefish boiled in water." By Conan Bryant Eaton

Story to be continued...

Ellison Bay is the second in a series of three books following the life of Bob Chadwick. The first in the series, Sandusky Bay, is available on Amazon and Nook in paperback and in e-book. The Sandusky Bay audio book is available for purchase on 2BRealMen.com. There's also free audio table talks on their website, where Jerry and Tom discuss every man struggles on the road to real manhood.

COMING...Book Three, the conclusion of the Chadwick Series

This is a preview. The number of pages is limited

LAKE OF BAYS
On Root Hog Island

JERRY PRICE & TOM ROY

Chapter 1

ON THE MEND

Bob Chadwick left Sandusky, Ohio, an angry man. He resented the close relationship between his wife, Lois, and Sandra, their teenage foster daughter. He felt stabbed in the gut by Sandra, who clearly threatened his authority as the man of the house. And after a few months of secret planning, he packed a few things in an old Ford, wrote Lois a note, and drove away from his life.

Nearly a year later, after settling in the tiny village of Ellison Bay in Door County, Wisconsin, Bob realized he could run but not hide from himself. His new friend Van had introduced him to Jesus, stirring Bob to look deeper into his soul. Now, it was time to return to Ohio to see if he could pick up the pieces and rebuild his marriage.

* * *

It was five hundred and sixty miles from Ellison Bay to Sandusky Bay in the old Ford. Bob knew he couldn't make that trip in one day but his expectation of talking with Lois made the miles fly by. He knew he had been a self-absorbed jerk, which was the Chadwick way. But the thought of learning to love and allowing himself to be loved made him come alive.

Bob left Ellison Bay as a man *on the mend* beginning to accept the blame for the appalling amount of pain he perpetrated in their marriage. His drinking and pornography resulted in untold marital harm.

Bob also carried some of his own hurt into his marriage. An abusive father and the paralyzing experience of sexual abuse in the urinal of a West Virginia coal mine had left him emotionally vacant and calloused. Then after the pain of losing Joey, their only son, he walked out on his wife. Right now, all he could think about was getting to Sandusky Bay and asking for Lois's forgiveness.

*   *   *

As Bob approached Sandusky, he decided to stop at the Ottawa National Wildlife Refuge. It would be a great place to step out of the Ford and do some serious thinking. The two-lane road into the preserve curved to the west and then crossed some open water.

Suddenly, a dark shadow moved across Bob's left shoulder.

Startled, he glanced up in time to see a huge black shape with a white head and a golden...*What the heck! A bald eagle,"* he yelled. Because the road was without a shoulder to pull over on, he just marveled at the sight, while the traffic behind him began to come to a halt. He craned his neck as the majestic bird passed only a few feet above him, headed for a marshy area at the edge of the lake.

Bob had never seen a bald eagle in Door County, although the peninsula had plenty of natural areas and rugged coastline. His friend Van told him the Native Americans, who had once inhabited the county, believed an eagle flying overhead was a sign of the Creator's blessing.

JERRY PRICE & TOM ROY

Could this be a good sign for him in anticipating his talk with Lois? Bob wondered if he'd ever be able to rebuild his marriage but the reason for this talk was to ask her forgiveness. As a new follower of Jesus, he was learning a new way to live.

A few minutes later Bob stopped in at an old bait shop for a soda pop. An enormous ginger colored tabby cat sprawled on the counter beside the cash register, lazily eying him as he paid for his drink. Bob paid and left quickly, hoping his cat allergies wouldn't kick in.

He found a picnic table and sat down to enjoy his soda, listening to a symphony of songbirds and thinking of his friend, Van. He had been honored when Van asked him to pray for him about his decision to work at a Christian men's boot camp on the Lake of Bays in Ontario, Canada. For Bob, that was a blessing and he began to pray for Van.

"God, I have a lot of things on my mind, as you already know. But my buddy Van needs help in determining what he should do, just like I do. I don't know what to say to you other than asking you to let Van know if he should take that job. I don't know how you do stuff like that, but would you do it?"

Bob hesitated and then continued, *"I don't know what's ahead for me either, but I want to repair my broken relationships. And I know Van is praying for me, too. So God, would you help me know what to say and do when I meet Lois and my friend Al? Thank you."*

Bob had no idea how much he would need God's help.

BOOKS BY JERRY PRICE & TOM ROY

BEYOND BETRAYAL
A Table Talk
Available in Paper Back

Can anyone doubt betrayal is a part of our human fabric? We can see it everywhere in epic proportions, depending on media coverage and personal experiences. Beyond Betrayal unpacks life after betrayal as authors Jerry Price and Tom Roy explore the twists and turns of a betrayer's identity. Contending with the wounds everyone faces in recovering from the impact of betrayal, they also examine God's prescription for healing. They take an unusual view of betrayal, seeing it as a core condition of mankind's heart or soulfulness. Beyond Betrayal avoids the quick, easy answers in order to navigate tough issues underlining the hurt and encourages discussion with reflective questions. Price and Roy challenge all of us to rebuild trust levels out of a hope that doesn't define anyone by the treachery of deceit.

SANDUSKY BAY
A Novel
Available in Paper Back and Audio

Sandusky Bay follows a generational journey of three men: a grandfather working the coal mines in West Virginia, his steel mill working son in Ohio, and a grandson growing up with the baggage of previous generations. Join the journey of these three men as they find themselves trying to navigate the worlds of work, women, family, and life's unexpected trials. "Sandusky Bay thoughtfully and creatively exposes the misconceptions of what many men have learned real manhood looks like. Through the characters in this story, you see both the good and bad potential of the decisions you make and how they can affect the ones who are following you through this journey on earth."
- Chris Singleton, ESPN Analyst

Visit **2BRealMen.com** for information about more books, *paper back and audio*, that both Jerry Price and Tom Roy have authored.

Ellison Bay 188

JERRY PRICE & TOM ROY